D0645472

# HannaH WeSt
## on Millionaire's Row

# HaNNaH WeST

## on Millionaire's

*A Mystery by*
**Linda John**

*SLEUTH*
PUFFIN

PUFFIN BOOKS

Published by the Penguin Group

Penguin Young Readers Group, 345 Hudson Street, New York, New York 10014, U.S.A.

Penguin Group (Canada), 90 Eglinton Avenue East, Suite 700, Toronto, Ontario, M4P 2Y3, Canada
(a division of Pearson Penguin Canada Inc.)

Penguin Books Ltd, 80 Strand, London WC2R 0RL, England

Penguin Group Ireland, 25 St Stephen's Green, Dublin 2, Ireland
(a division of Penguin Books Ltd)

Penguin Group (Australia), 250 Camberwell Road, Camberwell, Victoria 3124, Australia
(a division of Pearson Australia Group Pty Ltd)

Penguin Books India Pvt Ltd, 11 Community Centre, Panchsheel Park, New Delhi - 110 017, India

Penguin Group (NZ), 67 Apollo Drive, Rosedale, North Shore 0745, Auckland 1311, New Zealand
(a division of Pearson New Zealand Ltd)

Penguin Books (South Africa) (Pty) Ltd, 24 Sturdee Avenue,
Rosebank, Johannesburg 2196, South Africa

Registered Offices: Penguin Books Ltd, 80 Strand, London WC2R 0RL, England

This Sleuth edition first published by Puffin Books,
a division of Penguin Young Readers Group, 2007

1 3 5 7 9 10 8 6 4 2

THE LIBRARY OF CONGRESS HAS CATALOGED THE PUFFIN SLEUTH EDITION AS FOLLOWS:

Library of Congress Cataloging-in-Publication Data
Johns, Linda.
Hannah West on Millionaire's Row : a mystery / by Linda Johns. — Sleuth ed.
p. cm.
Summary: Pre-teen sleuth Hannah West gets caught up in a mystery involving feng shui and
missing antiques while housesitting in a mansion on Seattle's famed Millionaire's Row.
ISBN 978-0-14-240824-7
[1. Housesitting—Fiction. 2. Mansions—Fiction. 3. Antiques—Fiction. 4. Feng shui—Fiction.
5. Seattle (Wash.)—Fiction. 6. Mystery and detective stories.] I. Title.
PZ7.J6219Hg 2007
[Fic]—dc22
2007015346

Puffin ISBN: 978-0-14-240824-7

Printed in the United States of America

For my sister, Nancy

SOMEHOW I MANAGED TO GET OUT OF MOST OF THE HARD WORK THE LAST two times we moved. Not this time. Neither did my best friend, Lily.

"I thought you and your mom were minimalists," Lily said, her voice a bit muffled as she struggled with an armload of blankets and a down quilt. "Free of possessions and all of that."

"I'm a collector now. I need room for my works of art and my bric-a-brac," I said, trying to sound haughty. I was, after all, moving into a house on Millionaire's Row. And at that exact moment I tripped.

Lily giggled.

"You'd trip, too, if you were walking sideways with a masterpiece like this," I said, thankful that I hadn't gone all the way down or damaged the corners of the three-foot-by-four-foot canvas I was toting up the walk to our new house. This massive masterpiece was a joint effort that my mom's friend Nina and I had been working on for months in Nina's downtown Seattle studio. We'd just finished it last week. I had to shuffle sideways instead of walking straight ahead because the painting was so huge.

I couldn't see Lily, my best friend in the whole entire world, but I could sense her eyes rolling at me.

"I remember the good old days when you'd boast about getting all your possessions into your car," she grumbled.

Lily was kidding, of course. I may have tried to make a joke about how everything Mom and I owned fit into our old Honda Civic, but those kinds of jokes really never turned out that funny. Technically, you could say that Mom and I are homeless. But we really aren't; we just don't have our own home. Things had been kind of rough financially for Mom the past couple of years, but then Mom had a great idea. After we lost our house, we started lining up jobs house-sitting. People go on vacations or long business trips, and they hire us to take care of their homes and their pets. We're lucky that it all works out for us. And Mom's lucky she has me, I keep telling her, because I'm the one who actually does the most to take care of the pets. She, in turn, reminds me that she knows how lucky she is.

So here I am, moving into a three-story house on Fourteenth Avenue East at the top of Capitol Hill in Seattle. I put the painting down in the foyer (that's what people in big houses call their entryways) and stepped back onto the porch to look down the tree-lined street. I'd read about the houses here being "stately," which, according to my dictionary, means "majestic; imposing in magnificence, elegance; dignified." That about wraps it up, although I'd add "old, huge, and gorgeous" to describe the houses I saw on both sides of Fourteenth. Lumber barons and other rich businesspeople in the early 1900s built their houses at the top of this steep hill overlooking downtown Seattle and Elliott Bay. The street quickly got the nickname Millionaire's Row. I wouldn't mind being a millionaire today, let alone in 1906. My mind started mulling over how to figure out what the equivalent of a million dollars back then would be to today's prices. It's times like these that I need to shut off my brain. I'd already spent several hours on the tenth floor of the Seattle Public Library downtown researching Capitol Hill and our new street.

I had a good feeling about this street and this job, especially when a woman across the street with short spiky hair waved to me. She was walking with a younger woman, and I assumed they were on their way to a yoga class. The younger woman had a long, thin tote—the kind that people use to carry their yoga mats—slung over her shoulder. The woman who waved was carrying a rolled-up purple yoga mat and a purple tote bag with a yin/yang symbol on it. She obviously had an excellent sense of sophistication and style. My purple T-shirt with the yin/yang symbol on it happened to be one of my personal favorites. I'm the kind of person who has a list of all-time favorite symbols, and yin/yang is consistently in my top three. You see it lots of places these days. It's a circular symbol, half black and half white, with a small dot of white on the black side, and a small dot of black on the white side. It's an ancient Chinese symbol that some people call the "tai chi tu". The yin and the yang represent two opposing, but equal, forces. Lots of people say it's male energy and female energy, but it's more complicated than that. I like what I know about the concept. I also like that it's something with deep Chinese symbolism that's become part of American culture. I like to think of myself the same way: I'm Chinese, and I'm sure I have deep Chinese symbolism pulsing through my veins, but my American mom adopted me, so now I'm also deeply immersed in American culture. Ah, who am I kidding? I just like the way the yin/yang symbol looks.

The women stopped so that the younger one could take off her apricot-colored hooded sweatshirt and tie it around her waist. Underneath, she had a lighter apricot-colored T-shirt that had a swirling design surrounding the word *om*. The yin/yang woman looked older than my mom (who is thirty-eight), but like someone my mom would be friends with. The om woman—whose long dark hair was in a thick braid that reached almost halfway down her back—looked like she was about ten years younger.

As they started off again, both women smiled pleasantly at me. The older woman (aka Yin/Yang Woman) called out "hello" and "welcome to the neighborhood" when she saw my mom.

"Looks like we scored a friendly neighborhood again," Mom said to me.

"We're kind of lucky that way," I said. We'd easily made friends with the neighbors at every house-sitting job we'd had.

Mom turned back to the car. "Two trips this time. We need to scale back," Mom said, winking at me and putting her arm around me. "Come on. Let's get our last few things out of the car."

"I'll just wait for you in the piano room," Lily called after us. That's right. Our house has a piano—and the piano has its own room. And that room has a curved outer wall with windows that look out onto the street. The piano is the only thing in the room, managing to show off just how stunning a Steinway grand piano can be. "The only thing cooler would be if it revolved," Lily had commented earlier.

Mom and I headed back to our Honda while Lily hammered out "Chopsticks."

I grabbed my favorite photographs and some more artwork out of the car, along with my two goldfish.

"The cats are looking at Vincent and Pollock with a little too much interest," I said, trying to shield my goldfish from the all-knowing eyes of Simon and Sport, the two cats watching us from the porch.

"You'll have to keep the bowl covered so that all the cats can't go fishing," Mom said. When she said "all the cats," she wasn't just talking about the two outside watching us now. This house was home to Reba, Dolly, and Jasmine, as well as Sport and Simon. That's five, count 'em—five, cats.

"It's going to be different not having a dog around all the time," I said. Our last few house-sitting gigs involved dog-sitting and some dog-walking in addition to house-sitting. As a result, I've built a fairly successful dog-walking business with plenty of referrals. But I liked the idea of getting to hang out with cats for a change. Every time I spend the night at my grandma's house, her cat, Smiley, sleeps on my pillow, snuggled up to the back of my neck. Maybe I could get all five cats to sleep with me.

I knew I'd still get a lot of canine time. We were staying next door to one of my favorite dogs in the world, Izzie. I met her several months ago at the Elliott Bay Animal Shelter. I volunteer there a couple times a month, and I was there the day that someone brought Izzie in. She had been horribly neglected. We cleaned her up and nursed her back to health. I got extremely attached to her over the several weeks she was at the shelter. Luckily, she was adopted by Libby and Calvin. Even more luckily, my supervisor at the shelter had told Izzie's new family how she and I had a strong connection. Libby and Calvin invited Mom and me over to their house to see how well Izzie was doing. That's when Mom heard about the Parkers' trip and that they were looking for house-sitters. And that's the happy story of how we ended up on Millionaire's Row.

"Maggie! Hannah! Welcome to the neighborhood!" Calvin, our new next-door neighbor and Izzie's new owner, pulled up in his black Mini Cooper. I couldn't see who else was in the car, but I could guess from the enthusiastic barks coming from the backseat. Calvin opened the car door and Izzie came bounding out. She rushed over to us, but used her good manners and sat expectedly, waiting for us to pet her.

"I missed you so much, girl!" I said, crouching down to give Izzie the attention she deserved. It had been only a week since I'd seen her last. Calvin and Libby also had a little girl named Rachel. They'd hired me to babysit her a few times, usually just for an hour or two as a way to break me in and train me. Libby said she was especially pleased that I had taken the babysitting class at Children's Hospital. We'd learned CPR, tips on safety, and ideas for keeping children entertained. I'd set up my own Babysitting Suitcase, full of art supplies, two lion puppets, a few little wood trains, and some of my favorite books. It was a modest assortment that paled in comparison to the books and toys lots of kids have. But the four or five kids I've babysat seemed superexcited to open what I called the "Special Day Suitcase."

"Libby and Rachel will be home soon," Calvin said. "Rachel is so excited to have you living next door. She asks every morning if it's finally the day when you're moving in so you can babysit her more often."

"I can't wait to babysit Rachel again!" I said. "I

know we're right next door," I said to Calvin, "but here's my card so you guys have my cell phone number."

HANNAH J. WEST
PET SITTER, DOG WALKER, PLANT WATERER
AND ALL-AROUND ERRAND GIRL
235-6628

I added "babysitter" to my card just last week, now that I had official experience and a few references.

"We're going to go for a walk soon, before another rain shower hits," Mom said. "I'm sure Hannah would love to take Izzie with us on our walk."

At the first mention of "walk," Izzie sat down and looked at Mom patiently, showing what a good girl she would be. The second time Mom said "walk," Izzie barked. Dogs are amazing that way. I've never met a dog who couldn't pick that word out of an ordinary conversation. Even on TV. The dogs I know will be lounging around, maybe even seeming sound asleep, while the weather forecaster talks about Doppler radar, wind chill, El Niño, record highs and lows, overcast skies, sun breaks, and chance of rain showers (we have crazy weather here in Seattle, so you might actually hear all that in one forecast). Then the weather person throws in, "Take an umbrella on your walk" or "Good time to walk your dog." In a split second, the lounging dog will be up off its pillow and heading to the front door. Some dogs I know, including a labradoodle named Mango, even grab their leashes off hooks, generously assisting you while also getting out the door faster.

"I need to put my fish away, but then could I come get Izzie for our w-a-l-k?" I asked, spelling out the word. Izzie still barked. (And they say dogs can't spell.) Dogs are amazing, I tell you. "I'll see you soon," I said, giving her a good scratch behind her right ear.

We told Calvin we'd come by and pick Izzie up in about twenty minutes. Mom and I needed some time to explore our house. Who am I kidding? We needed time to explore our mansion. After all, we're living on Millionaire's Row.

## CHAPTER 2

I RAN INSIDE TO PUT MY THINGS DOWN AND TO PUT VINCENT AND
Pollock into their bowl. It was going to be a challenge
finding a place that the cats couldn't reach. I dragged
a kitchen bar stool over to the refrigerator, climbed
up, and carefully placed the fishbowl on top. I gave an
admiring glance to the refrigerator. It was one of those
ones they call side by side, with the refrigerator on
the right and the freezer on the left. Lily's family had
one just like it. You could get crushed ice, cubed ice,
slivered ice, and cold filtered water without opening
the freezer door. Being able to get crushed ice with
the push of a button never gets old to me. The rest of
the kitchen was pretty amazing, too. Gleaming black
granite countertops contrasted with bright white cabinets. Everything was sleek and polished. The kitchen
looked like a showroom, mostly because there wasn't
anything on the counters. Not even a toaster. There

11

were so many cabinets and pantries that all the appliances were hidden.

"It's not forever, guys," I said to my fish. "I'll figure out a better place tonight." Simon, a part Siamese cat, was staring at me, twitching his tail. The top of the fridge didn't seem so safe anymore. I grabbed two vases and began setting up a makeshift wall around the bowl to protect it. The vases were superheavy. Even if one of the cats did get up there, it wouldn't be able to get to the bowl.

"It looks like you're building a fortress for Vincent and Pollock," Lily said, handing me another vase.

"I am. It's temporary, but necessary. Izzie's home, and we're going to take her on a walk so we can check out the neighborhood before it rains." I hopped down from the stool. "Want to look around the house before we go?"

"Mom's picking me up any second," Lily said. "But I do want to see some of this monster house before she gets here. I know she's dying to see it, too, but we have to go get The Brother from a birthday party, so she'll have to wait." Lily was on a kick of calling her little brother, Zach, who is actually pretty cute and not completely annoying, The Brother or, sometimes, Oh Brother. I think Zach secretly liked it.

I was excited to act as a tour guide and show off this huge house to Lily. We started in the sunroom, which is kind of like a porch but it's all glassed in. It overlooked the street and also, Mom had told me, would catch the morning sun. The owners, Happy and Frank Parker, told us they liked to sit out there in the morning and drink coffee, read the newspaper, do crossword puzzles, and watch the world go by on the street below. A loveseat with deep, red cushions, two chairs, and a coffee table made it seem like the kind of place you could stretch out and really relax. I'd already scoped it out as one—just one—of the many great sketching and reading spots in the house.

The main floor of the house had a living room, dining room, kitchen, office, and, of course, the piano room. That might not sound that extraordinary (except how many houses have piano rooms?), but each room was truly spectacular, mostly because of the size, the twelve-foot-high ceilings, the wood trim, and the immense windows. We headed upstairs, a trip that was impressive on its own. The wood staircase and gleaming wood banister are the kind you see in movies when the beautiful girl in an evening gown descends the stairs to the admiring glances of the roomful of dignitaries and royalty below. Halfway up the stairs was another choice reading spot: a long—at least eight feet long—cushioned window seat that was an ideal lookout to the neighborhood.

I took Lily up another flight of stairs to the third floor.

"This floor is off limits to us," I said to Lily, trying to sound ominous and mysterious. But I couldn't sustain the act, so I just opened the door to a weight room and workout area. "If you go through that door, you get to Frank's home office. He's an import/export guy, whatever that is."

"Don't they trust you up here?" Lily asked, eyeing the treadmill, rowing machine, and rows of weights.

"I was just kidding. They said we could use the equipment. I think this used to be where the servants lived, a hundred years ago. Because"—I paused while I opened what looked to be a closet door—"this is a secret staircase. It goes back down to the second floor, and then to the kitchen. This way the servants could get up at the crack of dawn and scurry down to the kitchen to make breakfast." Lily followed me down a flight of stairs, where we opened two other doors until we got out to the second floor hallway.

There were five bedrooms on the second floor. Mom said I could have first dibs this time, since there were a couple of house-sitting jobs where I ended up sleeping on the couch. This Capitol Hill house had so many bedrooms that we could each take two, and still be able to keep the master bedroom untouched until Happy and Frank returned. You might expect me to take one of the smaller rooms and leave the most deluxe for my mom. But if you expect that, you'd be wrong.

"Here's my new pad!" I said, swinging the door open to a guest suite. That's right. Not just a guest bedroom—but a bona fide suite, complete with a bathroom, walk-in closet (makes you wonder how long they expected guests to stay in the old days), and a "conversation area" with a love seat and two chairs. The bathroom itself was bigger than most apartments. Not only were there two sinks, but there was a whirlpool bathtub with steps leading up to it, a separate six-foot by six-foot walk-in shower (the measurement was Mom's guess when we toured earlier), and even the toilet had its own room. My bed was king-sized, with a thick mattress and so many fluffy quilts and pillows that there was a step leading up to it.

"Can you believe it?" I asked Lily.

"It's like you have your own apartment, minus the refrigerator," Lily said.

"No fridge, but there is an electric tea kettle and a Japanese tea set," I said. "Besides, Mom would never ever let me eat in a bedroom."

I showed Lily the three other bedrooms, and then gave her a quick peek into the master suite, which was, if you can believe it, bigger and better than my guest suite.

"Now this is the best part," I said, opening the last door in the hallway.

"There's more?" Lily asked. "I can't believe it."

I really had saved the best for last. At least it was the best in my opinion. In addition to five bedrooms, the second floor had an art studio. It wasn't huge, but it was absolutely perfect.

"Voilà!" I said, in my best attempt at sounding like a French artist. "And guess what? Happy said I can work in here!" This was my idea of heaven. An entire room devoted to sketching, painting, and creating whatever you wanted. The room was directly above the piano room on the first floor, which meant it had the same curved glass window overlooking the street. Did I mention the fireplace? It didn't look like they used it much. My first clue was that instead of a grate and firewood, the opening was filled with a statue of an elephant. A big cushy chair and ottoman sat next to the fireplace, with floor-to-ceiling bookcases on either side. Happy had her own art library, along with a couple of shelves of travel books. Yet another place for me to hang out, read, and sketch.

"Is that a painting one of the owners did?" Lily asked.

"Yep. This is Happy's studio. Most of the paintings in the house are hers," I said. "Mom is completely ecstatic to be living here. She loves Happy's work."

Lily examined the signature on the painting. "But that name looks like it starts with a 'J.'"

"Her real name is Josephine, but she's been called Happy since she was little. At least that's what she told me. She also said that I'm welcome to work up here and use her supplies. She showed me where everything was and how to take care of things here," I said. "Ouch! Why did you do that?"

Lily had pinched my right arm.

"I wanted you to be sure it wasn't a dream," she said. "Oops, there's my mom down in front. I know she wants to see all of this, so I guess I'll just have to come back to your mansion tomorrow," Lily said. "Ta-ta. That's what you rich folk say, right?"

"I think we prefer 'cheerio,'" I said, walking her down to the front door.

"What, ho!" Lily tried to get in the last word.

"I'd settle for 'later,'" I called after her.

It was time for Mom and me to go for our traditional Get-to-Know-the-Neighborhood Inaugural Walk. Luckily, it still wasn't raining. I ran downstairs to check on Vincent and Pollock again. I didn't think any of the cats could get through to them now.

A fluffy white cat sat demurely by the entrance to the sunroom. "We're all going to learn to get along, aren't we, Jasmine?" I said, petting her between her eyes.

Reba, Dolly, Simon, Sport, and Jasmine were all inside now. I glanced up at my goldfish again, even though I was pretty sure they were safe.

"They'd better be here when I get back," I called to the five cats, as Mom and I headed next door to pick up Izzie.

## CHAPTER 3

WITH IZZIE WALKING BETWEEN US, MOM AND I HEADED NORTH ON Fourteenth Avenue East toward Volunteer Park. Every house we walked by seemed to be more magnificent than the last, getting taller and bigger as we got closer to the park.

I'd been to Volunteer Park lots of times, but usually to go to the Seattle Asian Art Museum or on school field trips to the Conservatory. I hadn't really walked around before.

"Let's go to the top!" I said when we first entered the park and came to the old water tower. When I was little, I was convinced that Rapunzel had once lived at the top of this round red-brick tower. I still thought that when I was six and Mom held my hand as we walked up the 108 steps (she counted) that spiraled to an observation area at the top where you can see all of Seattle, from Lake Washington to Elliott Bay.

I love running up the stairs to the top, even if I do feel a little sick when I look down. "Oh, wait. We probably shouldn't go up with the dog."

Mom agreed and promised we'd have plenty of time to check it out some other time. We got to the art museum, where two camel statues flank the entrance to the museum. They're the kind of statues you just can't resist: they need to be touched, patted, and, most of all, climbed on. I handed the dog leash to Mom and ran up the steps and hopped on the back of one of the camels. Two little kids ran up after me, and then screeched to a halt as their mom said, "Wait your turn." I remembered how much fun I'd had on the camels when I was younger. (Who am I kidding? I still have fun on the camels. I imagine I always will.) I cheerily gave up my seat between the humps.

We walked around the reservoir, then back up the hill to the Volunteer Park Conservatory, a Victorian glass house where they grow cacti, orchids, banana plants, giant bird-of-paradise, and all kinds of other exotic and tropical plants that simply wouldn't grow in Seattle without TLC and a greenhouse.

"Sometimes I sneak up here in February when I'm tired of the winter rain and the gray sky," Mom said. "It feels so good to go from damp cold into the tropical air inside, or into the cactus room, where it's eighty degrees."

"You should bring me with you more often," I said.

"I will, especially now that we're so close. I promise lots of trips to the art museum, the water tower, and the greenhouses," Mom said.

"Cool!" I cried out. But I wasn't responding to her offer.

I could see tombstones on the outer edge of the park.

"I didn't know there was a cemetery here!"

"You've been there lots of times," Mom pointed out. "That's the cemetery where Bruce Lee is buried." She was right. I had visited his grave before, but I didn't realize that it was so close to where we were house-sitting.

Bruce Lee was a Chinese American from Seattle who is possibly one of the most famous martial artists of all time. He created jeet kune do, which is kind of like kung fu.

"This is so incredibly cool! Did you even notice what T-shirt I'm wearing today?" I lifted my Chavez Ultimate hoodie (my sweatshirt from my ultimate Frisbee team at Cesar Chavez Middle School) to show Mom my T-shirt underneath. Chinese characters surrounded a red symbol on a white background. The loose translation is something like "using no way as way" or "having no limitation as limitation." It was the symbol that was used in jeet kune do.

I love Bruce Lee. He starred in a bunch of martial arts movies like *Fists of Fury* and *The Chinese Connection*. I've seen all his movies. I'm not a huge martial arts fan, but I like that Bruce Lee was one of the first famous Chinese people in America. I would like him even if I weren't Chinese American, but I think I especially like him because he and I are both from China.

"Another place we'll come back to when we don't have a dog with us," Mom said. "We'll bring flowers, too." Bruce Lee's grave always had lots of flowers. You could easily spot his burial site all the way across the cemetery because there were usually at least a couple of people there to honor him.

We took a walk past the cafés and shops on Fifteenth Avenue East and looped back to Millionaire's Row. We truly had it all living here: big house, beautiful park nearby, coffee shops just a block away, not to mention being within walking distance to Bruce Lee's grave.

Calvin's black Mini Cooper passed us, and Izzie started pulling on her leash, as if she was going to run after it. The car pulled over in front of their house. Calvin got out with a bag of groceries.

"Good girl, Izzie!" Calvin said, taking the leash from us. "Thanks for walking her." He shifted the grocery bag to his left arm and started fumbling to get his wallet out, as if he was going to pay me.

"It wasn't official dog-walking business," I said hurriedly.

"Izzie was our excuse for getting out and walking around the neighborhood," Mom added. "We like to get to know the area where we're house-sitting as soon as we can after we move in."

"We'll make sure you know the neighbors, too," Calvin said. "There's our Block Watch captain now."

A woman in a brown velour jogging suit headed toward us, her forehead wrinkled up as if she were mad. Or confused.

"Grace? Is everything all right?" Calvin asked her.

"I just got back from my walk and . . . and I think someone has broken into my house."

## CHAPTER 4

**"ARE YOU OKAY?"**

"What was taken?"

"Have you called the police yet?"

Calvin, Mom, and I were all talking at once. I pulled out my cell phone just as Mom said, "Hannah, call the police."

"No!" the woman said.

Silence.

"No, please don't call the police! At least not yet. It's, it's . . ." her voice trailed off.

"Grace, what is it? Do you think someone is still in the house?" Calvin asked.

"Has someone threatened you?" I added.

"No . . ." her voice trailed off again. "I don't think anyone is there. And nothing seems to be missing."

"How did the burglar get in? Is there any sign of forced entry? Broken glass, maybe a jimmied lock?"

24

I asked. As usual, my mom turned and gave me that "Keep quiet!" glare.

"No. I can tell that no one forced his way into my house," Grace said.

"Or her," I said. And I got that glare from my mom again. "His or her. The burglar could be a female."

The woman smiled for the first time. "I think he—or she—wasn't really a burglar. I shouldn't have even said that someone broke in. That's too strong of a statement. More like someone . . . visited."

"You had a visitor? And nothing is gone?" I hoped my voice conveyed that what I really meant was: What the heck is the problem then? Mom gave me another glare.

This interrogation was driving me crazy. Why didn't this woman just come out and tell us what was wrong and why she thought someone had been in her house. This time I slowed myself down, with no intervention from Mom. This wasn't an interrogation. We hadn't even officially met this woman yet.

"I know it sounds insane, but I'm sure that someone was in the house because things look different," Grace said, talking to Calvin.

"Did someone leave something inside your house? Something icky?" I interjected. (You can't keep a good detective down when questions need answering.)

"Nothing's missing. There weren't any threats. It's so embarrassing, but I think someone came into my house and . . . and . . . cleaned it up."

"Cleaned your house? That sounds like the kind of burglar we could all use," Calvin said, starting to joke until he saw the look on Grace's face. "I'm sorry, Grace. I still think we should call the police. There was an intruder in your home. You, of all people, should know how important it is to report things. You tell us that all the time at our Block Watch meetings."

Grace agreed to let Calvin make the call to the police. She must be really committed to being Block Watch captain because she had the police precinct phone number memorized, so she didn't have to tie up 911 lines with a non-emergency call. I handed Calvin my phone just as Mom rushed into an introduction.

"I'm Maggie West, and this is my daughter, Hannah. We're house-sitting for Happy and Frank Parker," Mom said.

"And taking care of their cats," I added.

"That in itself is a big job! Imagine, five cats," Grace said. "It's nice to meet both of you, although I'm afraid this isn't the best way to welcome you to the neighborhood."

"It is an unusual way to meet our neighbors," I said.

Calvin ended the call and said the police would come to Grace's house within the next thirty minutes. "I'd wait with you, Grace, but I need to be downtown in a half hour."

"I know you don't know us yet, but I'd be happy to wait with you," Mom said. Grace looked relieved. It would be kind of creepy to go back into one of these huge houses knowing that an uninvited guest had just been there—and maybe still was there. Unfortunately, I sort of said that out loud.

"It's kind of creepy to go back into a big house right after a B and E. The intruder may even still be there," I said.

Once again, my mother glared at me.

But Grace laughed. "You certainly speak the lingo, talking about a breaking-and-entering offense. I'm sure everything is fine, but, just in case, I would certainly appreciate the company."

GRACE LIVINGSTON LIVED DOWN THE BLOCK IN A TWO-STORY WHITE house with a wrap-around porch. The porch was like an outdoor living room, with big comfy-looking couches and chairs, a coffee table, a wrought iron and glass table for eating, a rocking chair, and a porch swing. It looked like the cover of one of those home decorating magazines.

Grace bent down and moved a potted plant a few inches. "I'm going to have to find a new place for my key," Grace said.

"You don't mean you hide a key outside?" Mom said. "Under a flowerpot?"

"Another embarrassing thing to add to my list." Grace sighed. "I'm afraid I do. Whenever my son comes home from college, he almost always manages to forget his key. We tried hiding an extra in one of those hollow rocks you can buy, the kind that have a secret

28

place for a key and then are supposed to blend in with your other rocks. But twice the gardener moved it and I spent fifteen minutes on dark, rainy nights lifting up every rock trying to find the right one. I had hoped that my new hiding place was so clichéd that no one would think a Block Watch captain would do something so unsecured."

I noticed an ACE Security Watch sticker on the narrow window next to the front door. "What's that sticker mean?" I asked.

"Nothing. I canceled the security system two years ago," Grace said. "Nora, our cat, kept setting off the burglar alarm every time she came in and out of the kitchen cat door. I'd hoped leaving the sticker up might deter burglars."

The porch was immaculate, except for a tiny bit of dirt near a flowerpot. "Did the intruder knock over the flowerpot?" I asked.

"It was upright when I got here. But that's the first thing I noticed. It looks like it was moved just a few inches. I assumed I'd forgotten that I'd moved it before my walk, even though I don't remember doing anything like that."

We followed Grace through the front door. The inside of her house was similar to ours—I mean, the

Parkers'—house. A grand staircase stretched up to a landing on the second floor, the dark wood gleaming and inviting a ride down the banister. She led us into the living room, which had two separate seating areas. It looked pretty tidy all right, but I guessed that if Grace had a gardener, she probably also had someone come and clean her house.

"Maybe we should make a list of what's different, Grace," Mom offered. "Take your time going around and see what you notice. Hannah and I can take notes."

Grace opened the drawer of an antique cabinet and took out two notepads and pens for us.

"I don't use this room much, so it never gets too messy. Yesterday was the day Dana came to clean, too," she started.

"Didn't you say it was cleaned up today?" I asked, confused because it now sounded like it had already been clean.

"I should have said tidied up. My house was clean, but things are . . . rearranged. Those two chairs used to be over there," she said, pointing. "That glass bowl was on the left side of the table. I'd left *The New Yorker* open to an article I was reading, but now it's stacked up with the other magazines. Oh! The magazines are in a different order."

"They're arranged by size," I said.

"And the stack itself is neater," Grace added. "Let's see. I'm sure this bowl of rocks and sea glass was on the side table next to the lamp. Oh! That's strange." She picked up a polished rock, about two inches long and one inch high. "This isn't mine." She held it out for us to see. The rock was black with a symbol etched into it. It looked like kanji, characters used in Chinese and Japanese. I quickly sketched the symbol. I'm studying Japanese at Cesar Chavez Middle School, and kanji is just one of three scripts used in Japanese. Each symbol means a specific word. There are tens of thousands of kanji symbols in Japanese. This one looked familiar to me, but I might just be thinking that because I wanted it to look familiar.

"Maybe your son or someone added the stone as a gift earlier than today," I suggested.

"I don't think so. This is my collection of sea glass we've gathered together on the beach at Whidbey Island. We always made sure that this was only sea glass, not pebbles or rocks, no matter how pretty they were."

A quick succession of raps on the front door interrupted our conversation.

"Seattle Police. We got a call."

## CHAPTER 6

MOM AND I STAYED UNTIL THE POLICE HAD MADE A THOROUGH SEARCH of Grace's house, inside and out. It takes a long time when your house is a gazillion square feet and, on top of that, it's more than one hundred years old, so it has all kinds of nooks and crannies for hiding. I listened to Grace give her statement to the two police officers, who, I noticed, weren't taking many notes. Neither one of them even wrote anything down when she told them about the mysterious rock appearance. They would have been more interested if something had disappeared, rather than appeared. But when you think about it, having something *appear* is much more mysterious and intriguing.

They gave her a lecture on safety and securing a house, and left a brochure behind called "Stay Safe at Home."

It was clear to me that this case was mine. It didn't seem likely that anyone else would believe a woman whose complaint was that her house was tidier and, on top of that, someone had left her a gift.

I wrote Mom's cell phone number on the back of one of my business cards and handed it to Grace.

"Too bad I don't have any pets that need sitting. And my son is already a sophomore in college," she said. "Perhaps I'll have a few chores and errands for you." She thanked us for being such good neighbors, and we headed back across the street to our house.

"I can't believe how big these houses are," I said, looking at a three-story brick house—complete with turrets and second-floor balconies—two doors down from Grace's and directly across the street from Libby and Calvin. I noticed a familiar-looking metallic ACE Security Watch sticker in a corner of a window. I hoped those owners were better than Grace at using their alarm system.

After dinner that night, Mom checked through the whole house, making sure that every window was securely closed and that every exterior door was double locked. "None of this 'hiding a key under a flowerpot' business for us," she said, as she handed me my copy of the house key and gave me her standard lecture on being responsible for taking care of the house. This was our job, Mom reminded me, and our clients count on us to make sure their house, their belongings, and their animals stay safe.

We both jumped at the sound of a clunk in the kitchen.

"Meow!" Simon, the biggest of the five cats, announced that he was hungry. We went into the kitchen to make sure everything was okay.

"Simon makes quite a racket when he goes through that cat door," I said. Mom was down on her hands and knees, presumably looking to see if the cat door posed any threat to our safety.

"I can't imagine anyone could get in here through that, could they?" she asked me.

"Nope," I said, picking up Reba in one arm and Dolly in the other and heading upstairs to my room. I was amazed that these two cats, named after country-western singers, were being so quiet and letting me hold them, especially at the same time.

I set my laptop on the desk in the bedroom. I pulled out the sketch I'd done of the symbol on the rock. I went to a kanji Web site and began searching for a match. I tried the word *peace*, but it wasn't a match. There are several thousand symbols used in kanji, but fewer than two thousand were used regularly. If it took all night, I would go through all two thousand. But first I'd try a translation site where I could type in English words and see the ideograms. I tried a few typical words that we Americans like to see in Eastern script: *earth*, *water*, *happiness*, *calm*, and, finally, *harmony*. "Ladies and gentlemen, we have a match," I said to the cats.

The symbol on the rock left for Grace Livingston was Japanese kanji for *harmony*. A stone with that inscription would be a nice sentiment and a kind gesture under normal circumstances. But not if the recipient didn't know how it got there.

I checked online and saw that Lily was online, too, so I opened a chat window.

"We might have a new case," I typed.

"What's with 'we'?"

"You and me. The ace team at solving crimes . . . "

"At solving crimes no one else cares about."

"Calling you now . . . " I typed and signed off.

"Too many words to type," I said when Lily answered the phone. I filled her in on what had happened with Grace Livingston.

"Creepy," Lily agreed. "But I read something about how forgetful adults are, and I'm not talking senior citizens and Alzheimer's. People in their forties and fifties are getting spacey. That's why there are all those infomercials on TV about boosting your brain power and improving your memory. I'm telling you, there's a memory crisis in America."

I wouldn't exactly call it a crisis, but I let Lily go on a bit while I double-checked the word *harmony* in different languages. I didn't really need to prove anything, but it was fun to compare and contrast the interpretations in style even within the same language.

"I'm still going to keep an eye on things. Grace seemed seriously spooked," I said.

Later that night, I woke up when Simon the cat jumped on my bed. "You're a big fat noisy guy," I said. I thought I heard something else. I tried to make my ears superaware so I'd hear anything out of the ordinary. Then again, I didn't know what was ordinary in this house yet. I tiptoed to the door and looked out in the hallway.

"It woke you up, too?" Mom whispered.

I screeched a little at the sound of her voice.

"Sorry. I didn't mean to startle you," she said. "It's just a creaky board on the third step." She demonstrated by putting her weight on and off the step. "Even a small cat like Jasmine sets it off."

"Okay, then . . . "

"Want to grab your blanket and sleep on the couch in my room?" Mom asked.

Sometimes I think my mom is a mind reader. This house was too big, and I wanted to be close to her.

Mom, me, and five cats all slept in the same room for the rest of the night.

## CHAPTER 7

AFTER THAT FIRST NIGHT OF SCARY NOISES (WHICH WEREN'T EVEN THAT scary), Mom and I quickly got used to the house. It was pretty easy to enjoy living in such luxurious surroundings. This was quite possibly the cushiest job we'd ever had. While I was at school that week, someone came to mow the lawn, someone else came to clean the house, and a third person came to prune the bushes in the front. Not much for us to do but sit back and relax. And take care of five cats.

I think I earned my keep with those cats, however. Feeding them was no big deal, but cleaning out three litter boxes twice a day wasn't exactly my idea of a good time. I'd been running a little late Thursday morning before school, so I'd skipped the morning kitty-cleanup routine. I was dreading seeing what was waiting for me in the afternoon as I walked home from the bus stop after school.

The garbage and recycling trucks had made their way down our street earlier in the day. One of my regular jobs when we house-sit is to bring the garbage and recycling out to the curb first thing in the morning on garbage day. As soon as I got home from school, I wheeled the cans back to their spots. To potential burglars, empty garbage cans are like a beacon that no one's home.

This neighborhood was so nice that the waste-management people put the garbage cans upright and put the lids on after they emptied the garbage. On lots of other streets you see the empty cans strewn about, usually on their sides, and often rolling over the curb and into the street.

I unlocked the door to the house, called hello to the cats, put my things down in the entryway, called Mom at Wired (the coffee shop where she works) to tell her that I was home. She reminded me to put the trash can and recycling cart away behind the house.

"I'm already on it," I said. I went to the sidewalk and secured the lid on the brown garbage can, and started wheeling it to the back. I saw people at two houses across the street doing the same thing. One woman looked up, and I recognized her as the woman with the spiky hair who'd been carrying the yin/yang tote bag the other day. She smiled, waved, and began wheeling the recycling cart to the backyard. At the brick house next door to her, her friend with the apricot hooded sweatshirt was doing the same thing. She looked across the street, but she didn't seem to see me. The three of us were like a cacophony (vocabulary word for the week) with our noisy, clunky wheels rolling on the pavement. I came back to get the green recycling container, which, luckily, was also on wheels. The apricot hoodie woman across the street was ahead of me, though. She already had the recycling can behind the fence and was closing the gate. I hoped to catch her eye so I could do the friendly, neighborly waving thing. But she didn't look up as she headed off toward Volunteer Park. The other woman must have gone back inside her house.

You know how sometimes what you don't see is what strikes you as odd? That's what happened. I headed back inside, then stopped and looked back across the street. Something was missing.

Garbage cans! On the east side of the street, the garbage and recycling cans were all put away. On our side, they were all (except for ours) still curbside.

It wouldn't make sense that everyone on the entire side of the street would already have moved their cans.

Grace Livingston's house was on that side of the street, and I knew she was still at work at the University of Washington. She'd made a point of telling us she worked until five every day.

Then again, maybe Grace and her neighbors had hired someone to put things away during the day while they were at their jobs. These people hired out just about everything, so why not pay someone to wheel your trash cans away?

It was weird, but not criminal. I decided to be neighborly, and I took Libby and Calvin's cans down their driveway to the outside of their garage. Then I went inside to face the litter boxes.

## CHAPTER 8

THAT NIGHT, DURING DINNER, MOM GOT A PHONE CALL FROM Grace Livingston. She was calling an emergency Block Watch meeting.

"You're not going to believe this," Mom said. "Two of the brick houses across the street had intruders today."

"Was anything stolen?" I asked.

Mom shook her head no.

"Let me guess: things were cleaner than when they'd left in the morning?"

Mom nodded.

"Did they find any gifts, like rocks?" I asked.

"Grace asked both families to look around for that specifically. There were rocks at each house. But there was something else. At each house, there was something even odder left behind," Mom said. "You'll never guess."

Whenever someone says "you'll never guess," something inside of me takes over and I turn into a Guessing Machine.

"A million dollars . . . a big-screen TV . . . a new bicycle . . . a hamster . . . a pony . . . a piñata . . . fresh flowers . . . "

"Bingo!" Mom said. "Fresh flowers at one house. You're coming with me to the meeting to tell what you saw with the recycling. It might be nothing, but it might be significant. Then you'll get to hear firsthand what was left at the other house."

I brought my sketch pad with me to the Block Watch meeting, which was being held next door at Libby and Calvin's house. The adults gathered in the living room. I volunteered to take care of Rachel, partly because I really like her and partly because I wanted an excuse to be on the fringe of the meeting so I could observe everything. Rachel and I set up some crayons and a coloring book at the dining room table.

"What are you going to color?" she asked, concerned that there was only one coloring book, and it was clearly meant for her.

"I have my sketchbook. I almost always have a book like this with me," I said, showing her some of my drawings. "This way I can draw or color or write whenever I feel like it." I couldn't tell if she was impressed because she was already busily intent on her coloring work. Izzie came in and curled up on the floor by my feet. I started sketching random things I saw, beginning with a blue vase that had a silver cut-out pattern on it that made it look like irises were growing all around the vase.

"The police officer who came to the house didn't even bother writing anything down," one man in the living room said.

"It's still a crime to enter someone's house uninvited, but they don't seem too concerned."

"They'd rather wait until it's too late, either something is stolen or someone is hurt," a woman added.

Everyone started talking at once. Grace quieted them all down. "It looks like everyone's here, so let's get started."

"Should we wait for Louise?" someone asked.

"She called me right before I came to say that she didn't want to miss her yoga class. She said something that sounded like 'ash-tango,' whatever that means," a woman answered.

"We can fill her in later. Perhaps we could hear from the owners of the two homes that were 'visited' today," Grace said, directing her comments to four people on the sofa.

Both had the same M.O. as Grace's intruder: No sign of forced entry, nothing missing. Furniture was rearranged, and piles of books and magazines were tidied up.

"Hannah may have seen something odd this afternoon when she got home from school," I heard Mom say.

All heads turned toward me and Rachel in the dining room. I stood up and cleared my throat. I'm not the shy type, but talking to a roomful of adults is always a little intimidating. "It might not be a big deal, but when I got home from school, around three o'clock, I noticed that all the houses on the other side of the street already had their garbage cans put away. Things just seemed out of balance, because the cans were still out on this side."

"Tony must have brought ours in," one woman said, but her husband was already shaking his head no.

"I assumed you did it when you got home from work," the man said.

"It's probably not a big deal. It just struck me as odd," I said. I could feel my face heating up with embarrassment. My mom has all this confidence that because I'm a visual learner it means that I notice things that others might not. "Maybe your neighbor in the house with the turrets took care of it. I saw her and another woman when I got home from school."

A man and a woman on the couch interrupted: "That's our house!" they said at the same time.

"Oh, I don't really know who lives where yet," I said. "Maybe it was your daughter? Or a friend? It was a woman in an apricot hoodie." I had a feeling they might not all know what I meant, so I quickly added, "A sort of light-orange hooded sweatshirt. She has long dark hair."

The couple looked at each other and exchanged "Do you know who that is?" comments.

"Maybe she was just helping out the woman with the short spiky hair," I said. "She was outside, too."

"Oh, that's Louise," the woman said, visibly relieved. "She's always doing nice things for people. She has a crazy schedule, so she's often home during the day."

"That explains it! I think the woman I saw at your house is friends with Louise," I said. I was alternately relieved and disappointed: relieved that it wasn't something creepy going on, and disappointed that I hadn't discovered something useful for this case.

"I'm sure that explains it. Maybe Louise felt like being neighborly and returning all the garbage cans and she asked a friend to help. Louise is like that: extremely helpful and bighearted," Grace said.

45

Everyone started talking. Once again, Grace quieted everyone down. I think they all realized that it's kind of a silly thing to get all worked up about. Still, it was weird.

As long as I was embarrassing myself, I might as well keep going. "I have one other question, if you don't mind. Do you use ACE Security? I noticed a sticker at your house." I directed my question to the couple who owned the house with the turrets, one of the two homes that had been broken into earlier today.

"No, we've never used a security company. That sticker was there when we bought the house, and it was impossible to get off," the woman said.

"There's an ACE Security sticker on my front door, too," said the man who lived in the other house that had been broken into. "I've tried everything to get it off without damaging the wood."

Interesting.

"Most houses on this street used to have ACE Security," a man said. "They probably all have stickers."

I wasn't sure if he meant that to be reassuring or not, but everyone seemed to be nodding.

"Does anyone have an active account with ACE Security?" I asked. No one did. Doubly interesting. I made a note of it.

People had been passing around the stones that had been left at each of the three houses. When they got to Mom, she handed them to me with a meaningful look. I knew exactly what she meant. I placed them on the coffee table to compare them. Each one had a different symbol, but now that I'd researched the first one, I could see that all three stones had Japanese kanji. I copied the symbols into my sketchbook.

"Is there anything else that seemed amiss in your houses?" Calvin asked the neighborhood group.

"There's one thing," the woman from the brick turret house began. "It's just a little thing, but I'm sure the toilet lid in the foyer bathroom was open when I left for work this morning. It was closed when I got home."

"Maybe Charlie closed it on his way out," someone suggested.

Charlie shook his head. "I left before Jodi and got home after her. If she says she left it open, it was open. She does it on purpose."

That's kind of a weird thing to say.

"I leave it for the animals," she said, turning bright red. "I'm not gross or anything. It's perfectly clean. We never use it as a toilet. I just have this fear that I'll be away from home and there will be an earthquake or some other disaster and I won't be able to get home to our dog and cat. This way I know they have water."

"That's weird," I said, not realizing I said it out loud at first. Then I was the one turning bright red. "I mean, it's not weird that you leave it open. It's weird that it was closed. It just seems like a totally odd thing to do, doesn't it?" My voice trailed off, but it didn't matter, because all the adults seemed to be talking at once. This gave me time to think things over. To me, it didn't seem at all unusual to keep a toilet lid open so their animals could have water. If anything, it was practical. We had the opposite instructions in our current house-sitting gig. We had to make sure all the toilet lids were closed. One of the cats, Sport, had a thing for water. His owners feared he'd dive into any water he could find and not be able to get out. It might be a crazy thought, but better to be safe, right?

I was lost in my own watery thoughts until I saw Jodi, my fellow animal lover, holding up four red squares, each about three inches by three inches. Everyone quieted down. Was this some weird meeting ritual, where a red card meant "stop and be quiet"?

Turns out the red cards had an even weirder meaning.

## CHAPTER 9

**"THEY LEFT A PAINT CHIP AT THE HOUSE?" LILY ASKED ME AT LUNCH THE** next day. We were standing in line to get our daily dose of burritos. People never believe me, but the burritos at our school are truly delicious. The school buys them from Trader Joe's, so they're actually the same kind of burritos most of us have at home anyway. There's just a stigma about school lunch food being bad. It turns out it doesn't have to be.

"Several paint chips," I said. The thief, or rather the *un*-thief, as Lily and I decided to call the culprit, had left paint sample cards—the kind you get in the paint aisle of the hardware store—in Jodi and Charlie's house.

"Maybe it was an accident and it fell out of a pocket or something," she said, grabbing a tiny bag of organic baby carrots. We headed for a long table where Jordan Walsh and some of our other friends were sitting. This was our best schedule ever, since we had first lunch, and it turned out that a bunch of our friends from elementary school had the same lunch. We sat together at the same table every day. After Jordan and I became friends, she started sitting with us, too. We spent most of our time trying to avoid making eye contact with eighth graders. Of course, next year we'd *be* eighth graders. We'd have to find something else to be insecure about.

"The un-thief is cleaning things up. It hardly seems like this type of person would make a mistake like that. Besides, these weren't random paint samples. They were all in the same color family. Plus," I said, pausing to emphasize my next statement, "they were taped to a wall."

I'd seen the paint chips, and they were all these deep shades of red. They had names like "Long Johns Red," "Cardinal," "Red Barn," "Firecracker," and "Heart-Pounding Red." Since our friends had heard part of our conversation, we all spent the rest of lunch thinking of paint names. (Siamese Kitten Brown, Bloody Gash Red, Poisonous Purple, Scabbed Knee Brown . . . you get the idea. Of course, Jordan had to throw in Crimson Lake, the color we had dubbed the red streaks in my hair.)

All of this color talk gave me an idea. I'd have to wait until I got home to check it out, though. The last three hours of the school day truly crawled by. A new house meant a new bus route, so right after seventh period I said good-bye to Lily and walked four blocks to the Metro bus stop on Martin Luther King Jr. Way. I waited for the Number 8 with Chandra and Ari, two eighth-grade girls from my gym class.

"We can wait for you by the lockers next time, and we can all walk here together," Ari said.

"Are you going to keep taking the 8?" Chandra asked.

I told them I'd be on the Number 8 for a few weeks. I like that they didn't ask questions, but maybe they didn't ask because they weren't that interested in a seventh grader. Still, I didn't want anyone to know that Mom and I didn't have a real home. And as much as I'd like to be rich, I didn't want anyone assuming that I really lived on Millionaire's Row. They got off the bus before my stop on Fifteenth.

As soon as I got home, I greeted the cats and checked on my goldfish. I'd moved Vincent and Pollock to a larger bowl with a custom-made metal screen over the top, thus protecting them from any kitty who might feel tempted to go fishing. Still, I'm a little paranoid about these two guys, so I checked on them several times a day. I think they appreciated the company.

It was Friday afternoon, and I had a couple of hours to myself before I went next door to babysit Rachel. I pulled out my sketchbook and looked at the symbols on the stones the un-thief had left in three different houses. I resketched them, just as a way to focus my mind. Drawing does that for me. Soon I was lost in drawing and shading things, until I really looked at what I'd done. In addition to the kanji characters, I'd shaded the page with different reds. I'd also drawn a diamond shape with the word *ACE* in capital letters inside it.

ACE! How could I have forgotten? A few online searches later, I decided to pull out the phone book and simply look up the company in the business listings. There were two columns of companies that had names starting with the word *Ace*, but none of those companies dealt with home security. I randomly picked a security company from the yellow pages. I felt like a classic detective from an old movie, looking for information in a phone book.

"Hello? I just bought a house on Capitol Hill," I said into the phone. I don't know why, but when I'm trying to sound like a grown-up on the phone, I stand up and begin pacing. "It used to have a burglar system, I mean an anti-theft system, and the sticker is still on the front door. I just hate having stickers, so I'd like to start service with that same company."

"No, it isn't your company. And I completely understand that this isn't something you would normally do, but I would be so appreciative if you could tell me how to get ahold of ACE Security Watch."

The reply wasn't quite what I'd expected. It didn't really matter since the people on Millionaire's Row didn't have active burglar systems. Apparently they wouldn't ever be active with ACE again. The company went out of business three years ago.

Maybe I'd have better luck looking at kanji. I picked up my sketch. The combination of the shades of red and the kanji reminded me of something . . . of something I'd seen recently. I closed my eyes and willed the original thing that had triggered my memory to pop back into my head. Sometimes it works, sometimes it doesn't.

This time it did.

I went to the reading area that Happy and Frank had set up in the sun porch. The coffee table held a stack of books. There it was: the second one down, a red spine with kanji. I pulled out *Feng Shui for Your Home* and paged through the book until I came to a photo of stones with ideograms. There they were: harmony, serenity, and simplicity. The same as the three stones left in our neighbors' houses. I turned to a chapter on color, skimming the type until the word *red* caught my eye.

"Red is an auspicious color. Consider using it on a south wall of an office or studio to increase creative energy and enhance prosperity."

I looked out the sun porch window to figure out which way was north and which way was south. Jodi and Charlie's house, the one with the turrets, faced west. Based on the way they'd described the scene, I was pretty sure that the red paint samples had been left on a south wall in the living room.

I flopped down on the bed to look through more of the book. Placement of flowers were discussed in another chapter. Still another had an extremely interesting passage:

"Career opportunities enter the home through the front door. If a bathroom is located near the front entry, be sure to keep the toilet lid closed when not in use. Otherwise, your opportunities could flow away immediately. Chi and fortune can be literally flushed away."

As I read that, I was struck by an obvious realization. Our un-thief was studying feng shui.

**I DON'T KNOW MUCH ABOUT FENG SHUI, EXCEPT THAT IT'S A CHINESE TERM** and it refers to the theory that where you place things in a room helps determine the positive flow of energy. I went to my favorite online dictionary and found this:

> *feng shui*: The Chinese art of positioning objects in buildings and other places based on the belief in positive and negative effects of the patterns of yin and yang and the flow of chi, the vital force or energy inherent in all things.

According to the little bit I'd garnered from paging through the book, someone who practices feng shui would pay attention to color, balance, and placement of things including couches, mirrors, and a bowl with sea glass in it.

Now I just needed to find someone locally who practiced feng shui and had a way of getting into other people's houses. That's all.

It was almost five o'clock. Mom wasn't home yet, so I called to let her know that I was heading next door for my Friday-night babysitting job. She made me promise to call when I got there, too. It's so embarrassing. Then again, having to call to check in so often was a small price to pay for all the independence I had.

Libby opened the door and Izzie came running to meet me, with Rachel close behind. Izzie sat down and looked at me expectantly. In one swoop I knelt down to hug Rachel and pet Izzie.

"Where's the Special Day Suitcase?" Rachel asked. She said "special" so it sounded like "spess-ul." So cute.

"It's on the front steps. Do you think you could help me bring it in?"

Rachel didn't need to answer. She pushed past me to get outside and grabbed the suitcase handle, proudly wheeling in my babysitter suitcase o' stuff.

"We're going to have so much fun tonight!" I said as Rachel led me by the hand into the living room.

Libby was going downtown to meet Calvin after work. They were going out to dinner and to a play at the Fifth Avenue Theatre. "We should be home by eleven o'clock. Rachel's bedtime is eight o'clock. The pizza just came. Lots of root beer in the refrigerator," Libby rattled off as she bustled around the kitchen/

family room getting her purse, her keys, and her jacket. She kissed her daughter good night and headed out.

"Let's eat pizza!" I said, gratefully noting that Libby had ordered from Pagliacci, my favorite pizza-delivery place. One half was plain cheese. The other was artichokes and mushrooms—my favorite! "How did your mom know what kind of pizza to get?"

"She called your mommy," Rachel said

This was a pretty sweet arrangement.

"Are you going to be in the parade tomorrow?" Rachel asked me.

"What parade?"

"The one that goes right down our street. The one that goes tomorrow. I'm going to be a firefighter in the parade," she said proudly. Could I love this girl any more? I've seen lots of four-year-old girls who are obsessed with being princesses. But not Rachel. She was a free-thinking preschooler who was going to some parade somewhere dressed as a firefighter. I couldn't think of any holiday or big celebration that would be happening that weekend. Maybe it was a neighborhood parade down on Broadway or up on Fifteenth.

After two games of Trouble and three hands of Go Fish, Rachel was ready for story time. Four times through *Skippyjon Jones* (featuring a Siamese cat who is convinced he's really a Chihuahua), and Rachel's eyes were starting to close. Izzie and I waited in her room until she was completely asleep, and then we quietly tiptoed downstairs.

"Ready to be my model again?" I asked the dog. I'd drawn Izzie several times when she was at the shelter. In fact, one of my drawings was in a frame on the wall here. She'd truly found the perfect home (especially since her new family appreciates fine art by moi). I got comfy on a couch in the family room and started sketching. My yearlong studio-art project at school was all about dogs. We did lots of other things throughout the year, but we were supposed to be working on one theme consistently during the year to see what kind of progress we made. The first drawings I'd done of Izzie focused on her and her alone. Maybe if I put some things from a family home into the picture I could signify that she now had a permanent place to live. I invited Izzie up onto the couch. I moved a photo of Rachel on the end table so that it was closer to Izzie. A vase on the end table would give some nice height.

"Wait a second," I said out loud. Izzie lifted her head slightly in case I said anything of interest to her. "This vase was in the dining room two nights ago." It looked good in its new position, but it also seemed a teensy bit dangerous to have this porcelain vase in a low, open area in a house with a rambunctious preschooler and a tail-wagging dog. When Libby had seen my sketch of it the other night, she'd told me how much she'd always loved that vase and how it had been her great-great-great-grandmother's.

I headed toward the dining room, with Izzie padding after me, to see if maybe there was another vase just like this one. But the vase I'd sketched on Thursday night was in the family room, not the dining room. A different vase, a bit taller, was in its place. I also noticed that the dining room table had been turned 90 degrees. The chairs were placed with two on each long side, instead of one on each of the four sides, as they had been the last time I was there. People rearrange their furniture all the time, but this felt strange. I couldn't tell if anything else was different. I scanned the hutch and the top of a dining buffet.

Next to a glass bowl of little oranges was a small black polished rock. I picked it up, already knowing what I was going to see. This time, I could even decipher the kanji. It was a character I'd seen several times while researching the other three stones.

This one said "energy."

## CHAPTER 11

I DID WHAT ANY TOP-NOTCH PRIVATE EYE DOES IN A SITUATION LIKE THIS:
I called my mother.

I had imagined how creepy it would be to know that someone was inside your house. Someone you hadn't invited. And now I was feeling it.

Two hours later, Libby and Calvin pulled into the garage. They came in through the basement and up to the family room. "We're home!" Libby called. "All boyfriends up here with Hannah better disappear—" She stopped midsentence when she saw my mom. A look of panic instantly took over her face.

"Everything's okay!"

"Rachel's fine!"

Both Mom and I started talking at the same time, knowing that Libby and Calvin would be obviously worried why their responsible babysitter had needed her mother to hang out with her. I could tell they still felt something was wrong, even after they checked on Rachel and kissed her while she was dreaming.

Libby came back to the kitchen and offered us tea. She has one of those contraptions in which you heat water in the morning and it stays the perfect temperature for tea all day. I'd seen this same thing at Uwajimaya, a Japanese market down in the International District/Chinatown. (People between the ages of forty and sixty tend to call that area the International District, which is what it was called in the 1980s. But it's really Chinatown, so now people do a slash when they talk about it. You know: a slash in the middle so that it's both things: International District/Chinatown.)

"Did you move the water, Hannah? It's absolutely no big deal if you did. It must have been heavy to move, though," Libby said.

"Nooooo, I didn't move it," I said.

"That's strange. I guess Calvin did this morning, and I was so busy all day I didn't even notice. Although I did make tea this afternoon ..." Her voice trailed off.

"Where is it usually?" I asked while I grabbed my sketch pad. I added "water contraption moved" to my list of odd occurrences.

"It's in the corner, between the wall and the toaster," she said. She was looking at the vase on the end table. Her face was scrunched up in a look I interpreted as puzzled. I looked at Mom. She nodded to me, a signal to go ahead. I took a deep breath.

"I don't know your house that well yet, but I was wondering about some other things that have been moved since we had that meeting last night," I said.

Libby plopped down on the sofa. Calvin, who had gone upstairs to change out of his suit and into sweatpants and a T-shirt, sat next to her and asked, "What's wrong?"

"Someone's been in our house. That's what you think, isn't it? Oh, dear! Was it tonight, while you and Rachel were alone?"

I didn't think it had happened while we were there. You'd think I'd pick up on it if someone had been moving furniture around in the dining room.

"I don't think so," I told her. "I was drawing Izzie tonight, and I noticed that vase was in the family room. I noticed only because I had sketched the vase last night when it was in the center of the dining room table," I said.

"Those pictures, the photographs," Calvin said. "Those were in the dining room, too, weren't they, Lib?"

Mom and I followed them into the dining room. "I don't suppose you and Rachel were rearranging furniture tonight?" Libby asked softly. I shook my head no.

"There's something else," I said. "The rock over by the satsumas. Was it there before?"

"Satsumas? Like little oranges?" Libby and Calvin looked at the bowl on the buffet. "We didn't have any satsumas."

Calvin picked up the rock and slid his fingers over the smooth surface. "I wonder what this symbol means? I wonder if it has significance?" he mused.

"I'm not positive, but I'm pretty sure it's Japanese kanji for 'energy.' I'll look it up tonight and let you know," I offered.

"I guess there's no point in calling the police, with the track record our neighbors have had," Calvin said. "On the other hand, I really think we should call them in the morning."

"The parade is in the morning, too. It will be crazy around here," Libby said.

"What parade? Rachel was talking about how excited she was for the parade, too, but I wasn't sure what she was talking about," I said.

"*Antiques Caravan*, that public television show, is rolling into town tomorrow. They're filming part of their opening sequence on Fourteenth Avenue to get some shots of historical houses in Seattle," Calvin said. "Rachel's extremely excited to be a firefighter on the sidewalk as the caravan passes by."

"It's not exactly a costume parade," Libby began, "but you know Rachel. Any excuse to dress up."

This was the first I'd heard about *Antiques Caravan* coming to town. It seemed it was news to Mom, too. Maybe everyone on the street had found out before we moved in.

Calvin walked Mom and me home, which Mom insisted wasn't necessary. Calvin said he always made sure Rachel's babysitters made it safely home.

It was after midnight, but I needed to get some answers. I got out my list of things that had been changed in Libby and Calvin's house:

Vase moved to family room

Family photos moved to family room

Dining room furniture rearranged

Bowl of fresh fruit (satsumas) appeared

Hot water container moved

Polished stone with symbol for "energy" added

I pulled out *Feng Shui for Your Home* and began looking for any possible meaning. I wasn't sure if the bowl of fruit was significant because it was food or because of the orange color. I wasn't sure where to start, so I paged through the book, looking for meaningful words to jump out at me.

*Family* was the first word to get my full attention. In that section I found this:

"The Creativity and Children area is located in the West corner of your home."

Their family room was in the back of the house, facing downtown, the water, and the west. Apparently this was a good area for family photos and personal items.

Perhaps the dining room was rearranged because of this philosophy: "You can change the flow of energy by moving your furniture around." The rock that said "energy" could be a token to remind us of the importance of energy and change. It was placed in the room where the flow of energy had been redirected.

Two things could explain the bowl of satsumas. Fruit represents abundance. I surmised that abundance in the dining room could represent a bountiful feast to keep the family healthy and nourished. I also read that the dining room should be the warmest room in the house, and one way you can warm it up is to introduce reds, golds, and oranges. The satsumas were doing double duty: as fruit they represented abundance; their orange color helped warm the room.

Much was written about electrical appliances. It was advised to not place water or a water source between an electrical outlet and an appliance. That could be why the toaster was moved to be right next to the outlet, and the water container was moved to remove interference.

It was one o'clock in the morning by the time I turned off the light. Luckily, the next day was Saturday, so I could sleep in.

## CHAPTER 12

**SO MUCH FOR SLEEPING IN.**

"Hannah, it's for you. It's Lily, and she doesn't sound happy," Mom said, handing me the phone.

"Hannah Jade West, I'm so disappointed that you didn't give me advance warning of the *Antiques Caravan* parade in front of your house," Lily started off, without even saying "Hello," "How was babysitting," or "So sorry to wake you up before noon."

"Huh?" was the only response I managed.

"My dad woke me up to show me the front page of the local news section. *Antiques Caravan* is doing a TV shoot on your street, as if you didn't know," she continued.

"Actually, I didn't know until—"

"I'm jumping in the shower now, and I should be there in a half hour. Maybe thirty-five minutes. I need to figure out what to wear," Lily said. "See you then."

I might as well get up and hit the shower, too.

*Antiques Caravan* is a superpopular show on public television. Once a week people tune in to watch other people find out if their family heirlooms are truly heirlooms . . . or just junk. It's pretty addictive to watch. Last week a man brought in an old map he'd found in his father's attic after his father died. The map was a 1928 Grizzly Gasoline Road Map of Montana. Just an ordinary map that you fold up and stick in your car's glove compartment. But this guy's dad had kept it neatly folded and stored in an envelope. The pristine condition, as well as the advertisement for a gas company that didn't exist anymore, made the map worth several hundred dollars. The man who now owned the map was ecstatic, even though he wasn't going to sell it right away.

That same week, a woman brought an ivory bowl that had been handed down through her family. She seemed confident that it was a true heirloom, worth a lot of money. Turns out it was simulated ivory instead of real ivory. In my opinion, that makes the bowl much more desirable. The thought of killing elephants for ivory is completely disgusting to me. Anyway, because it wasn't real ivory the bowl was valued at a few hundred dollars, not the thousands of dollars the owner had been expecting. Turns out that the map of Montana and the simulated ivory bowl were worth the same amount. One person was thrilled about it, the other sorely disappointed. Kind of funny how it all turned out. I'm sure there's a life lesson in there.

Each episode of *Antiques Caravan* opens with shots of the city they're visiting. They're called "establishing shots" because they establish the location with images of the city skyline and landmarks. They also try to show some local color. An old-style truck trailer with the *Antiques Caravan* logo leads a parade down a residential street in the old section of the city. I guess this time our street was the one they were going to use to showcase older homes in Seattle. This was the "parade" that Rachel had been so excited about.

What to wear for a parade? Let's see. How about jeans, high-tops, and my school ultimate Frisbee sweatshirt (the one that said "Chavez Ultimate"). Cool, but classic. I pulled the sweatshirt off soon after I'd put it on. I went to the closet and grabbed my mom's old Washington State University sweatshirt that had the cougar mascot's head on the front. It was vintage and cute—and added a certain local flavor to the *Caravan* crowd. Maybe it would earn me a second or two on TV.

I ran down the stairs when the front doorbell rang.

"I'll get it!" I called out to Mom. I swung the door open, ready to say something utterly witty and sarcastic to Lily, but when I opened the door I saw a firefighter. A little one.

"Hi, Hannah. Are you coming to the parade?" she asked.

"I hope this isn't too early to stop by," Rachel's mom said. "Rachel insisted that we make sure you were up and ready to go to the parade."

"Teenagers sleep too late on Saturdays," Rachel said.

"I'm up and I'm ready. I don't have a firefighter uniform, so I decided to wear a cougar," I said. Rachel nodded, like she was giving me her approval, so I went on. "My friend Lily is coming over, too. Do you want to come in and have some hot chocolate and wait for her?"

Rachel nodded again and marched her little firefighter self into our house and toward the kitchen, calling for the cats as she went. "Jasmine! Sport! Simon! Reba! Dolly! Here kitties, kitties." She'd obviously spent time in the house and with the cats before.

Mom invited Libby in for tea, and the two of them went into the living room to talk. Rachel and I hung out at the kitchen bar counter on "the tallest stools" (as Rachel called them), sipping our cocoa and talking about different waving techniques for parades.

"I like this one," Rachel said, enthusiastically shaking her hand back and forth.

"How about this one?" I moved my left and right arms in an interpretation of a stop-motion animal.

Rachel giggled. "You look like a robot! Now I'm a princess, waving to my royal kingdom." My little fire-fighter friend did a quite impressive imitation of one of those beauty queens with fake smiles and tight, sparkly dresses who always appear on at least one float during a traditional parade.

"There's also this one," I said, extending my hand at a right angle and moving it in circles clockwise, then counterclockwise.

"Wax on, wax off," said Lily as she walked into the kitchen. We burst into giggle fits and continued "wax on, wax off," which is funny only if you've seen the movie *Karate Kid* seventeen times like we have. When I try to explain why this is absolutely hyster-ical, I usually get a polite "Oh, that's nice" comment. This time, Rachel giggled along with us, caught up in our laughter.

"Love the outfit, Rach," Lily said approvingly. She looked at me, sort of smirked, and added, "Always so nice to see you, Hannah."

"Love your ... boots" was all I could come up with in

return. "I gather you're dressing in a historical fashion today?"

Lily was wearing a straight light brown linen skirt that reached midway down her calves. She had on dark brown tights and black leather ankle boots that laced up the front. A beige linen top was tucked in under a three-inch wide suede belt. A brown cardigan and her hair in a French braid were the final touches to her vintage look.

"The houses on this street are mostly circa 1901 to about 1915. I believe I've achieved a modicum of success dressing appropriately for that era," Lily said. Just then her cell phone rang, which kind of negated the historical authenticity of her getup. I mean, "outfit."

"Is it time?" Rachel asked, pointing to the clock above the stove.

"Yes, it is! Let's hit the streets," I said, helping her off the bar stool.

**CHAPTER 13**

**"I GUESS THAT GUY OVERSLEPT," I SAID ONCE WE WERE OUTSIDE.**
A man in his bathrobe was running down the street after what I presumed was his car, which, at that moment, was hooked up to a tow truck. The rest of the street was clear of parked cars.

The street looked wider and more majestic without cars parked next to the curb. The lack of cars really helped show off the towering oak and maple trees, while also opening up the view to show off people's front yards and houses.

The sidewalks were lined with people on both sides of the street. It looked like there was a good crowd along the parade route all the way down to Volunteer Park—about a five-block length. I recognized several people from the Block Watch meeting.

"If this had been just one week earlier, it would have been a parade to celebrate our moving in," I said.

"I'm glad you moved here," Rachel said, still clinging to my hand.

"Hannah, if you have time to let Rachel stay with you during the parade, I know she'd be thrilled. We'll consider it babysitting. Will that work for you?" Libby asked.

"Deal," I replied.

"I'll be nearby if you need anything," she said. "Oh, and here's a key in case you need to get into the house for anything," she added. I could tell she was relieved to be able to mingle with the neighbors on the sidewalk without constantly keeping an eye on a child. I've done lots of babysitting jobs where the mom or dad is in the house or in the yard, but just wanted a bit of a break. In fact, I had a couple of jobs as a "mother's helper" (even though it was really with a dad who ran a business out of his house, but no one says "father's helper") even before I took the babysitting class at Children's Hospital.

I looked around the small crowd, wondering if I'd see anyone from school. I saw the spiky-haired yin/yang woman, Louise, moving through the crowd, shaking hands and giving something to people. The younger woman with the apricot sweatshirt was there, too. She smiled as Louise introduced her to people. She looked across the street and waved to me and Rachel, too. I did one of those quick look-arounds to make sure she was waving to us before I waved back.

A white Ford F-something pickup (one of the really big kinds) was driving slowly down Fourteenth. A woman stood in the back talking into an amplified megaphone. She was far enough away that I couldn't hear what she was saying. As the truck moved closer, I saw the familiar *Antiques Caravan* logo on the hood and the driver's-side door. The truck stopped in the middle of our block.

"Thank you for coming out on this glorious morning!" the woman's voice came out loud and clear, without any annoying buzzing or crackling. "We're so happy to be bringing *Antiques Caravan* to Seattle, Washington!" People began cheering.

"Thank you, thank you," she continued. "Now, let me tell you a little of what we're going to be doing. The first time the *Antiques Caravan*'s caravan," she paused for laughter, "will lead the parade heading north. A camera person will be walking alongside the sidewalk to capture your genuine excitement about the arrival of the caravan. Now that will be our first run-through. There will be at least one more. During the second one, the first vehicle you will see will be our camera truck, just an ordinary Ford pickup with cameras. The main camera will focus on the vehicles; two auxiliary cameras will, once again, capture your genuine excitement about the arrival of the caravan. And you will be genuinely excited, because the second time through our *Antiques Caravan* host Marcia Wellstone will be driving the truck, with cohost Bradford Hines in the passenger seat. We also have some guests from a local car club. Please relax and have fun! Thank you!"

As she talked, a man passed out a sheet of paper that outlined basically what the megaphone woman had just said. It also showed the parade route. After our part, with "genuine excitement," was completed, the camera truck was going to continue into Volunteer Park to capture images of the water tower, the Seattle Asian Art Museum, and the Conservatory.

The truck moved to the next block and stopped in the middle. "The first time the *Antiques Caravan*'s caravan will lead the parade ..." I could hear bits of the same speech we'd just heard.

"What's it say? What's it say? Can I have it?" Rachel asked, looking at the orange flyer I held.

"It shows where the cars and trucks are going to go during the parade and after the parade," I said. I turned it over. The backside listed the dates and procedures for trying to get an item appraised and featured on *Antiques Caravan*. Starting on Friday morning, people could bring their treasures to the Washington State Convention Center downtown. For two days, appraisers would screen the items. I handed the flyer to Rachel, who intently studied it as if imitating me when I read it.

"We totally have to be there on Saturday morning so we can get on the show. I think I have a good shot at getting selected," Lily said, smoothing the front of her linen skirt.

"Lily, it's not about you. It's about the items and their value. It's about whether your necklace or lamp or vase has a good story behind it," I pointed out.

"Nonsense. Personality and camera presence always come into play, not to mention clothing choices and a sense of style. Besides, I can make anything have a good story," she said.

An old-fashioned car horn *toot-tooted*.

"It's starting!" Rachel said, jumping up and down.

Indeed it was.

## CHAPTER 14

MORE HORN HONKING. FRIENDLY *TOOT-TOOTING*, NOT AT ALL LIKE THE obnoxious horns on new cars and trucks.

We cheered and waved as the *Antiques Caravan* old-style panel truck came down the street. We kept waving for the camera. A black antique car followed. A sign on the door said "1914 Ford Model T." Underneath it said "Lake Washington Antique Car Club." Eleven more cars followed, all from the same car club.

One camera guy with a handheld camera came toward us to get a close up of firefighter Rachel. She tipped her fire hat, then reached over to give Izzie a big hug.

"Now that's a shot that's going to make it on TV," I whispered to Lily.

"Rightie-o," Lily said a bit loudly with one of her English accents. She succeeded in getting the camera guy's attention and he zoomed in on her, then backed away to get Rachel and Lily both in the shot. By default, I figured that my vintage cougar sweatshirt and I might also have a chance at being on TV.

"And yet another shot guaranteed to make it on TV," Lily said to me in her regular, nonaccented voice. She looked pretty smug about the whole thing.

"Hey, Chief," a college-aged guy with a clipboard said. "Just in case we use a picture on the show, we're going to need permission from your parents."

"I'm the babysitter," I said. "I'll get her mom over here."

"We may need one for both of you, too," he said.

"Of course!" Lily cooed, smiling warmly. "We've been through this before, haven't we, Hannah, dear?"

Luckily, I didn't need to be embarrassed because the clipboard guy had already moved on and hadn't paid any attention to Lily's pompousness.

The parade itself was pretty anticlimactic. It was over in five minutes. We'd have to wait at least ten minutes for the caravan to circle around and get back for the second run-through.

Rachel pulled my hand. "Hannah, I have to go. Now," she said.

"Can you hold it?" Lily asked. "The parade is going to start again soon."

"That's a little insensitive," I said, glaring at Lily. "She's only four," I mouthed.

"Now," Rachel said, tugging my entire arm with urgency.

"Okay. When you gotta go, you gotta go," I said to Rachel. "We'll be right back," I told Lily.

Rachel was moving a little slow for a kid who was desperate to go to the bathroom.

"Let's hurry," I urged her. The unspoken part of that sentence was "before it's too late." Of course, Rachel has been potty trained for at least a year, but I learned in my babysitting class to take a child's request to go to the bathroom quite seriously.

"I'm okay," Rachel said.

"What? Don't you have to go?" I asked.

"Yeah, I do. But it's not an emergency or anything," she said. "I'm going to need help. You'll need to hold my fire chief hat and maybe my coat."

Apparently Rachel the Firefighter was planning ahead to avoid an emergency during the parade.

"Hi," I said, a bit surprised to see the young woman in the apricot hoodie coming down the driveway on the other side of Libby and Calvin's house.

"Oh, hello," the woman said. Neither of us said anything for a few seconds too long, which always makes me nervous and leads to my talking too much.

"I'm house-sitting at the Parkers'. But now I'm babysitting. You live on this street, right? Louise's neighbor? I'm Hannah, by the way," I said.

"I'm Rachel. I'm a fire chief," Rachel said, following my lead and introducing herself.

"I'm quite pleased to meet you, Chief," the woman said, holding out her hand for Rachel to shake. "My name is Georgia, and it's nice to know we have emergency staff here on such a busy day." She shook my hand, too, as I introduced myself.

"We're just running home to use the bathroom," I said.

Georgia looked at me, then realized I was waiting for her to say something. "Oh, right! I was just checking the iron. Ralph was afraid the iron was left on, and I volunteered to run over here and make sure it was turned off. It was. Off, that is. It was off. Ralph lives alone, and you know how things like that can be troubling. But all's well. I'll see you two back at the parade," she said.

Rachel giggled.

"What's so funny?" I asked. I was a little alarmed that the giggle might indicate we hadn't made it to the bathroom in time.

"She called Mrs. Rosetto 'Ralph.' That's silly!"

"Maybe Mr. Rosetto is Ralph?" I said, unlocking the front door to her house.

Rachel stopped laughing and looked at me very seriously. "There isn't a Mr. anymore. Mrs. Rosetto was really sad. Too sad to have trick-or-treaters. Now we won't have noisy ice cream at our picnic."

I speak Four-Year-Old, so this all made sense to me. Apparently Mr. Rosetto had died some time before Halloween. He must have brought homemade ice cream to a neighborhood picnic. He probably made it in one of those contraptions where you have to keep cranking it. Lily's dad did that, too. He was always trying to get us to help crank, but we didn't fall for that one anymore. It was a lot of effort for a little bit of ice cream. And Rachel was absolutely right: it was noisy ice cream.

Rachel handed me her hat as we ran down the hall to the bathroom.

"Emergency! Emergency! Coming through!" she screamed, adding a wee-wooh, wee-wooh sound like a fire truck. Once we took care of business, we headed back out to the parade. I'm always careful about locking the door when I leave a house, but this time I was hyperaware of being careful and making sure everything was locked.

"I need to take this to your mom so you can be on TV," I said, walking Rachel's permission form over to Libby. She and my mom were talking with Louise, the yin/yang woman, who smiled when she recognized me.

"This is my daughter, Hannah," Mom said, by way of introduction.

"We haven't formally met yet. I'm Louise Zirkowski," she said, extending her hand. I like it when grown-ups shake hands with me. "I live in the red house across the street. I believe you and I share an interest in tai chi tu."

I smiled, impressed that she said tai chi tu instead of yin/yang. Even more impressed that I knew what it meant. "I just met your friend Georgia at"—I didn't actually know whose house it was now— "at the Rosetto house?" I finished my sentence as a question. I hate it when I do that, but I really was questioning whose house Georgia had been at.

"Really?" Louise's forehead furrowed. "That's odd. Did you say Ruth Rosetto's house?"

"Yeah, she said she was just checking on something," I said. Ruth? Ralph? They sounded kind of the same. Maybe Rachel and I had heard Georgia wrong and she hadn't said Ralph after all.

Louise closed her eyes and appeared to be taking deep breaths. Then she opened her eyes. Her face looked relaxed again.

"Maggie, let me give you my card," Louise said, handing Mom a business card. "You may not need my services, but perhaps you know someone who does. I'm fairly new at it, but I believe I have quite a knack."

"May I have a card, too?" I asked. "I collect them."

"Of course!"

Louise Zirkowski handed me a card advertising her services. Below two familiar-looking symbols were the following words:

*Louise Zirkowski*
*Feng Shui Specialist*

**"FENG SHUI?" I ASKED, SURPRISED BY THE COINCIDENCE.**

"Are you familiar with it? You pronounced it correctly," Louise said appreciatively. I said it "fung schway." I knew that wasn't absolutely positively correct, but it's as good as most Americans can get.

"I've read a little bit. I don't know that much, but I like to learn about Chinese traditions," I said.

"We should talk sometime, Hannah. In the meantime, I should get back to the other side of the street. Our instructions for today ask that we stay roughly close to the same place in each take."

I showed the card to Lily, who seemed to register the significance of the symbols right away.

"Can I hold it?" Rachel asked, apparently wanting to hold the business card. I couldn't take my eyes off of it. There was kanji above the words *feng shui.*

"Sure. I'd really appreciate your taking good care of it. It would be really supercool of you if you let me

84

have it back when we go home," I said. Rachel nodded solemnly, carefully holding the card and then putting it in her pocket.

"Here we go again," Lily said, pointing to the caravan.

A boring white pickup led the way, just as the megaphone woman had said. Next came the *Antiques Caravan* truck. I recognized the main host from the show, who was driving and waving. I recognized the man in the passenger seat, too, although I didn't know the names of either one today.

"Who are they?" Rachel asked, giddily jumping up and down and waving to the hosts.

"Marcia Wellstone and Bradford Hines," Lily said.

"Hi, Marcia," I called with the crowd.

"Hi, Marcia! Hi, Marcia!" Rachel followed my lead. Once again, the camera guy was right there to get a shot of Rachel. "Hi, Georgia! Hi, Georgia!" Rachel waved energetically to Louise and Georgia across the street. Louise nudged Georgia and pointed toward Rachel. A woman with a camera perched on her shoulder turned to get crowd shots across the street.

Louise smiled and waved for the camera just as her friend Georgia backed up and stepped behind a taller man.

Must not like TV for some reason. The exact opposite of my two companions, the fire chief and Miss 1906.

## CHAPTER 16

"WELL, THAT WAS AN EXCITING MORNING," LILY SAID WHEN WE GOT inside. She stopped in the entryway to unlace her boots and kick them off. She grabbed a duffel bag. "I'm going to change my clothes in your room."

Sometimes Lily may seem rude, but she's not. I like the way she doesn't need to ask for permission at our house (or wherever we're house-sitting), and I don't need to at her house. It's like each of us is part of the other's family. It's nice.

"While we're up there, let's think of something to bring to *Antiques Caravan*," she said as we climbed the stairs.

"Good idea," I said. "It's too bad we have to go to school on Friday."

"I know. That means Saturday is our one and only chance to be featured on the show," Lily said.

"Featured?" I asked, raising one eyebrow (a trick

that I'd just mastered). I headed out the bedroom and down to the art studio, with Lily right behind.

"Of course. A couple of young girls like us with a family heirloom? Who could resist?"

I had put some of my own art supplies out with Happy's brushes and paints. I picked up my own brushes and took them out of the pot. "I know!" I exclaimed triumphantly. "This!" I held up my brush pot for Lily to examine.

"I love this pot!" she said. "It's so cool that your grandpa gave it to you. But I think we should come up with something showier."

"Nope. I'm bringing this." I had made up my mind. My mom's dad had died of cancer before Mom adopted me. But he had known that I was coming because Mom had been waiting eighteen months to adopt a daughter from China. He didn't really know about *me*, specifically. But he knew he would have a granddaughter someday. He had left a gift-wrapped box for my mom to open when she came back from China with me in her arms. Inside was a Chinese porcelain pot to hold calligraphy brushes (or, in my case, paintbrushes) and a small companion piece to rest a brush on. They were both robin's egg blue. The pot had a border at the top in green. Mom said it was as if her dad had predicted I'd be an artist.

"Hmmm . . . You do have kind of a good story there," Lily said. "I'm going to have to find something equally sentimental, but more valuable. I can't imagine that my parents have anything, but if they do, I'll find it."

After Lily left, I took out Louise Zirkowski's feng shui business card. It didn't take long to find the meaning of the characters. Next to the yin/yang symbol was the kanji for "tai chi tu." But this was Chinese kanji, slightly different than the Japanese kanji stones left in people's houses.

Feng shui is pretty popular. It was silly to think there was a link to the break-ins and Louise Zirkowski. Right?

**CHAPTER 17**

ON TUESDAY, LILY AND I WENT TO THE SEATTLE PUBLIC LIBRARY DOWNTOWN right after school. I love going to the library, especially the downtown one. It's an eleven-story building that has this weird shape on the outside and lots of glass everywhere. An architect named Rem Koolhaas designed it, a fact I like to throw in because it's fun to say his name. It's not what you expect of a library at all, yet it's full of books, so it immediately feels comfortable.

If I have enough time, I like to go to the reading room on the tenth floor. It feels kind of like a modern cathedral, basked in light. It's quiet and comfy.

Today we didn't have lots of time. We were on a mission. We headed to the Teen Center on the third floor and got on computers right next to each other.

"Oops, that's too many," Lily said. She had found hundreds of results in the online catalog when she typed in "antiques."

"Try something like 'antique guidebook,'" I suggested. Still too many books to look through. We wanted to find some sort of guide that might give us a clue if our items were worth enough money to actually get on *Antiques Caravan.*

After we narrowed our search, we headed up the escalator to the fifth floor.

"Can I help you?" a man asked. He probably assumed we wanted a computer. There are more than one hundred computers on that floor. But there's also a bunch of reference books.

"We want to research values of antiques," I said.

The librarian took us to a shelf and pulled out three books for us. "This is a good general place to start. We have dozens more on the eighth floor, so if you're not finding your item, we'll look up there, too," he said. "These books have been very popular this week because *Antiques Caravan* is in town."

"It figures," Lily muttered. "Everyone in Seattle is probably trying to get on the show."

Everyone probably was. We'd preregistered online, which gave us a number and a time to show up. Lily, me, and our moms were going Saturday morning at ten.

I opened a book called *Kovels' Antiques & Collectibles* and found the section on porcelain. It looked like my brush pot and brush rest might be from the Ming Dynasty (1368–1643). Of course, they could also be imitation. My grandfather had left me several letters, and he never said anything about the origins of the pot. They are beautiful and precious to me no matter what. Still, it would be kind of cool to know how much they were worth. I wonder if that makes me ultramaterialistic.

"Wow! Let's find one of these!" Lily said. "Listen to this: jade and gold jewelry box estimated at eighty *thousand* dollars. Do you have one of these lying around?" She showed me the picture.

"Gosh, we don't have one just like that. Wait! Look at that vase," I said, pointing to another photograph. "That looks like the one Libby has. She said it was from her grandma."

We made a photocopy of that page to show Libby. I wanted an excuse to go to their house anyway. I needed to finish my drawing of Izzie on the corner of the couch.

We took the escalator down, stopping on the third floor and then the first floor. We stopped at the Teen Center for us, and then at the Children's Center to get picture books. I picked some to read to Rachel, and Lily grabbed a couple for The Brother.

Neither Lily nor I can leave a library without a book or two—or nine.

Mom made me wait until after dinner to call next door. As soon as Calvin heard my voice on the phone, he invited me over for cocoa. I asked if I might be able to draw Izzie some more and he said, "You bet. We'll make it a double cocoa."

I wasn't going to babysit, but I had a hunch Rachel would be disappointed that I wasn't bringing the Special Day Suitcase. I grabbed a coloring book from the suitcase and a box of sixty-four crayons. I'd tell her it was a Special Art Day.

Mom walked me over. As soon as Calvin opened the door, I could smell the cocoa. It smelled delicious. It wasn't just ordinary instant cocoa: this was Mexican hot chocolate, my absolute favorite.

"Thanks! It smells so good, like the kind I get at Wired," I said, heading over to the counter and cradling a mug in both hands. I took in a good chocolatey whiff, just like I do at Wired Café where Mom works.

Mom laughed. "It *is* the kind you get at Wired."

Libby held up a canister of Wired Cocoa. "We love it. Thank you, Maggie."

"Well, you're welcome. But it was intended as a

thank-you for helping us get this house-sitting job, not as Hannah's personal supply," Mom said.

Mom said good-bye, and Calvin promised to walk me home later. Then he turned to me.

"Can we see what you have so far?" Calvin asked, nodding toward my sketchbook.

I opened my sketchbook to show them, and then eagerly took another sip of my drink.

"Oh, Hannah, this is lovely," Libby said. "It conveys right away that Izzie is a part of our family."

Wow. That's exactly what I was trying to do. Cool.

"I'll help you re-create the pose," Calvin said. "Izzie, you lucky girl. You get some couch time." He patted the couch and Izzie obligingly hopped up, and then plopped into the corner.

"I moved the vase back to the dining room, but I decided those photos looked nice on the table here," Libby said. "I'll get the vase for you."

Rachel settled next to me and we began our Special Art Day projects.

"Calvin, could you come here a minute, please?" Libby said. My ears pricked up. Her voice sounded a bit tense.

"Are you sure you put it there?" Calvin said, speaking softly. "When was the last time you remember seeing it? Has the cleaning service been here? Are you sure it's gone?"

I couldn't resist. I put down my sketchbook and headed to the dining room.

"Is everything okay?" I asked.

"My vase. It's gone," Libby said, looking around as if it might suddenly appear.

A police siren broke the strained silence. Flashing red and blue lights pulsated through the dining room window. We all ran over and looked out, just as a second squad car pulled up. The officers jumped out and went to the house directly across the street.

## CHAPTER 18

"WE'D BETTER STAY IN HERE," CALVIN SAID. "WE DON'T KNOW WHY THE police were called. It might not be any of our business."

Calvin, Libby, and I stood at the dining room windows, our eyes transfixed across the street.

I jumped when the doorbell rang. Calvin opened the door to let my mom in. I had a feeling she didn't like being in that big house all alone when something was happening across the street.

I jumped again when the phone rang. It was Grace, starting the Block Watch phone tree. Grace called Libby, and then Libby would call Louise, and Louise would call the couple next door, they'd call someone else, and so on.

"I need to call Louise, but let me tell you quickly. Someone broke into Mark and Tom's house. Their Chihuly bowl was stolen," Libby said. I'd never been inside Mark and Tom's house, but I know that Dale

Chihuly is the best-known glass artist in the world. He lives in Seattle, but he's famous well beyond this city. A Chihuly bowl would be extremely expensive.

"Anything else missing?" I asked.

"Not that they've noticed so far," Libby said, dialing a phone number.

Calvin pulled out his cell phone. "I'm calling the police about the vase," he said. Libby nodded in agreement as she started talking with Louise.

"The dispatcher is sending one of the officers from across the street to talk with us," Calvin said.

"We don't need to stand here and watch those obnoxious lights. Let's all go back into the family room," Libby said.

Mom and I offered to stay for a while. We could help distract Rachel while Libby and Calvin talked with the police. Two officers came. One asked for permission to walk the exterior of the house to look for signs of entry. The other asked about the vase itself.

"Do you have a photograph of the vase?" the officer asked.

"No. Actually . . . Hannah, could you bring your sketchbook?"

It was already open to the drawing of Izzie with the vase. "Nice," said the officer. "Too bad it isn't in color."

I turned back several pages to the first drawing I'd done of the vase. I'd done that one with my Prismacolor pencils.

"That's perfect," Libby said. I offered to tear it out for them.

"Now, what can you tell me about the vase. Age, material, value?" the officer asked.

"I don't know much about it," Libby began. "It used to be in my grandmother's bedroom. I'd always loved it, so she gave it to me when I graduated from college. I'm afraid I don't know much more."

"I do," I said. I had completely forgotten to give Libby the photocopy from the book that showed a vase like hers. I pulled it out of the back left pocket of my jeans and unfolded it. I handed it to Libby, who passed it on to the officer.

"You certainly seem to have a keen interest in this vase," the officer said. She looked at me for few more seconds and then wrote something in her notebook.

I was about to tell the officer what else I had learned about the vase when I noticed her looking at me funny. Suddenly, I had a feeling that I had gone from being helpful to being a suspect.

## CHAPTER 19

"THERE'S CERTAINLY A LOT TO TALK ABOUT AT TONIGHT'S BLOCK WATCH meeting," Mom said during dinner the next night.

"Didn't they just have one? Geesh. How often do these people meet?" I complained because I knew that is what people expect from a twelve-year-old girl. But I already knew there was a regularly scheduled Block Watch meeting. In fact, I was eagerly anticipating it in case I could get any more clues about Libby's missing vase.

"Oh, stop," Mom said, clearly seeing through me. "You knew this meeting was scheduled. Didn't Libby already ask you to babysit?"

"Well, yeah. And I'm planning to stay close by again. I want to hear everything they discuss."

"I would expect nothing less of you," Mom said.

The meeting was at Calvin and Libby's again. We headed next door about fifteen minutes before the meeting started. I could start playing with Rachel and get her interested in some art project, and Mom could help Calvin and Libby put out trays of cookies and coffee.

Neighbors came in groups of two and more, opening the door and calling out "hello" as they did. Nice and friendly, but in my opinion things were a little too friendly considering that a series of thefts were happening on this street. Louise slipped in silently, mouthing "hello" to me and moving gracefully to sit on a cushion on the floor. I could picture her meditating in a similar position.

"This is great. We're all here tonight!" Grace began. "Thank you all for your cooperation during the *Antiques Caravan* parade. We have a lovely letter from the producers of the show, as well as some delicious Dilettante Chocolates, which I'll pass around for all to enjoy." Grace paused and looked around the room. "We have some tough topics to address tonight. Before we get to the theft at Mark and Tom's house, how about if we recap some of the odd things we've noticed in the past couple of weeks."

"I'm curious by what you all mean by 'odd,'" Louise said.

"'Odd' seems a bit mild," one man said. "It's a crime for someone to enter someone else's home. Sure, it's odd if things are rearranged, but the act of entering uninvited is well beyond odd."

"Did the rearranging appear to be an improvement?" Louise asked.

"Are you joking?" the man replied.

"Actually, dear, it did seem nicer when we came home," a woman said, patting her husband's hand as if to calm him down.

"That's not the point!"

"Clutter can create chaos and stagnant energy in our living spaces," Louise said, although I think most people—except me—had tuned her out.

"My house was tidier and my toilet bowl was closed. Remember?" Jodi said. "Tell me that wasn't odd." She said it in a breezy way, but I could tell she was still freaked out about the possibility of someone being in her house. As soon as she stopped talking she started biting her nails. I looked around at the Millionaire's Row dwellers to see what kind of nervous tics others might have. I could see the tension on people's faces. Everyone's except Louise's. She looked relaxed and content.

"It's worrisome to think of anyone being in your house or your private spaces," my mom said to the nail biter. I could tell Mom was trying to comfort her.

"How about if we hear from Mark and Tom," Grace said. She was a good leader. She stayed calm and kept the conversation moving. People seemed to respect her.

"I felt like something was off before I noticed that the Chihuly bowl was missing," Tom began.

"What do you mean by 'off'?" Calvin asked.

"I don't really know how to explain it. There seemed to be subtle changes, such as a chair moved at a slightly different angle."

"I hadn't moved anything, and neither had Tom," Mark said. "We called Geoffrey, our cleaning guy, but we didn't really think he had any insight into it because he hadn't been there for several days."

"What kind of changes?" Louise asked.

"Well, in the kitchen the coffeepot was moved so that it was closer to the sink," Tom began, but Louise interrupted.

"Was there anything between the sink and the coffeepot?" Louise asked anxiously.

"No. It was right next to the sink," Tom said, looking at Louise as if to say, Why are you asking such a completely weird, random thing?

Louise crinkled up her forehead as if something was worrying her. Why had she asked about the sink and the coffeepot? A mental image of Libby's kitchen counter popped into my head. That happens to me a lot: an image just pops into my head. Sometimes it takes me a while to figure out what it is I'm supposed to see in the image.

"Electrical can't be right next to a water source," Louise said softly, walking into the dining room. She wasn't talking to me. In fact, she wasn't talking to anyone, except maybe herself.

I pictured the sink in Libby's kitchen, and how the electric teakettle had been moved. My mind whizzed back to Happy's feng shui book and a paragraph I had read that said to place an object between a water source and an electrical source.

"Is the feng shui wrong?" I whispered to Louise.

She looked startled. "Yes. It's the opposite of feng shui. Very bad chi."

Did this mean that whoever was breaking into houses was anti–feng shui? (Or would that be un–feng shui?) Louise couldn't be the culprit. I could tell that she was so passionate about the art of placement that she would never do it incorrectly.

"Louise, we're going to make a comprehensive list of any strange occurrences. Could you come back into the living room?" Libby asked quietly. Louise nodded.

Calvin was taking notes on his laptop. "We have four separate break-ins and two missing items. Anything else missing? Have you noticed anything, Louise?"

"Missing?" Louise seemed to hesitate before she said no.

The grown-ups wrapped up their meeting, promising to keep in contact with one another and to keep an eye on all of their houses. Grace made sure that the cell phone and work phone numbers were all up to date. As people headed out, I maneuvered to be closer to Louise.

"Are you sure nothing is awry at your house?" I asked her. "You seemed a bit distracted earlier." I was impressed with my straightforward approach tonight.

"I may have misplaced something," she began. "I'm sure I'll find it soon. My son and grandson were here last week with their dog. It could have been moved. Or even broken by Ollie's wagging tail." I gathered that Ollie was their dog. Brilliant deductive reasoning, isn't it?

"I really am interested in learning more about feng shui. Right now I'm confused about why someone would break into a house to feng shui. You would never do something like that . . ." my voice trailed off because I wasn't really making a statement nor was I asking a direct question. Besides, I got sidetracked wondering if "feng shui" could be used as a verb.

"I don't break into people's houses!" Louise said. "That kind of intrusion would interfere with the chi."

She didn't exactly answer my question. Then again, I didn't exactly ask her the question.

## CHAPTER 20

**THERE WERE NO MYSTERIOUS FENG SHUI VISITS OR BURGLARIES ON** Millionaire's Row the rest of the week. That in itself seemed strange. Why the sudden stop? Did the thief think we were watching too closely? Mom was certainly watching me closely. If she's at work, I always call when I get safely home after school. This week, however, she insisted that I not only call when I first got to the front door, but that I keep talking to her the entire time I'm unlocking the door, going into the house, and turning off the alarm system. Happy and Frank's house was about the only house without an ACE Security sign—and also about the only house that actually had a working alarm system.

At long last, it was Saturday morning and time to head to the Convention Center for our chance to get one of our items appraised on *Antiques Caravan*.

Lily, me, and our moms carpooled downtown

together. We could have easily taken the Metro. We even could have walked. But we needed the car because Mom was bringing a rather unwieldly object to the show.

I thought I would be embarrassed that my mom was carrying a lamp around, but we saw people hauling chests of drawers, cabinets, and other kinds of large furniture. There was a stash of grocery-style carts and flat carts for people to use.

The lamp belonged to Happy and Frank. They called to apologize for not telling us about the parade. When Mom said I was bringing something to the first-round appraisal, they asked if she thought it would be interesting to take something of theirs. I think what they were politely saying was that they had many valuable things in their house, and maybe we'd have a better chance to get on the show with one of their items. I thought for sure Mom would choose a piece of artwork, but here she was, carrying a table lamp.

"Lucky numbers 433, 434, and 435," Lily said. "I feel pretty good about those numbers." She was dressed, once again, in what she now called her "circa 1906 outfit." She had one addition to the outfit this time: a brooch that her mother had hidden away. The women in her family had handed it down to their daughters over the years. Lily's mom decided it was the right time to pass it on to her own daughter, making Lily the sixth to own it. "I never knew it was this old," Lily had told me earlier in the week on the phone. "I always thought it was just some dorky pin my mom wore on Thanksgiving and when we visit my grandparents." This morning Lily was wearing it proudly.

I counted about fifty-two people ahead of us. Our assigned time was eleven o'clock, with a suggested arrival time of ten o'clock.

"I read something that said that *Antiques Caravan* is an extremely popular show in prisons," I said. "Seems like pretty good thinking for those criminal minds. Gives them all kinds of ideas of what to steal when they get out."

"Why don't you girls go to Starbucks and get us some coffee?" Lily's mom said, handing Lily a twenty-dollar bill. Mom nodded, which surprised me. She likes to stay loyal to small coffee shops like Wired, where she works, and usually steers clear of big chains. But there was a Starbucks right in the Convention Center, so I guess convenience won out.

On our way back, I checked out the crowd, trying to guess who would make it on TV and who wouldn't. I was pretty sure Lily was doing the same thing. As I looked around, my eyes stopped on one particular individual. She wasn't wearing the same apricot sweatshirt this time, but I recognized Georgia, the Om Woman, right away. I pointed her out to Lily.

"That's Om Woman? I thought she'd look more zen and serene," Lily commented. She was right. Georgia was downright fidgety today. I thought she was alone, but then Louise joined her, handing her a cup of coffee. I hoped it was decaf, because Georgia was practically jumping from foot to foot. Like many others waiting for their shot on *Antiques Caravan*, they had a grocery cart for carrying their treasures.

We were lucky we didn't have to move any heavy objects. Mom was still hanging on to that lamp with one hand, holding her green tea with another. She raised the lamp a bit, which I realized was her attempt at a wave at Louise.

Louise bustled over.

"I didn't realize I'd see so many people I know here," Louise said.

"Isn't it amazing? Just think of all the treasures and interesting stories these people must have," Mom said.

"I suppose everything is a treasure if it has meaning to you. The problem is, people have so many things these days that they don't know what's important to them in life—or even in their belongings. Their acquisitive natures lead to all sorts of stress. They go shopping to buy things and then find themselves surrounded by chaos and stress because now they need to take care of all these *things*," Louise said.

"We are rather acquisitive, aren't we?" I added. I'm not exactly sure what that means, but it was fun to say it and sound smug.

"Yes, and less is always more," she said.

"I guess that's the feng shui way," I added.

"Just shui 'no' to clutter," Lily added. We all groaned a little at that one.

"I love your necklace," I said, admiring the yin/yang symbol that hung on a silver chain around Louise's neck.

There was a rumble of an announcement over the P.A. system. "I didn't quite catch what that announcement was, but I'd better get back to my friend Georgia and our place in line," Louise said. "As always, it's lovely to see friends and neighbors."

"You think she did it, don't you?" Lily whispered to me.

"What makes you think I think that?"

"You were doing that thing when you want to keep someone talking. 'We are rather acquisitive, aren't we?'

Come on. That's not something you say every day. Or *any* day."

"Yeah, I do think she did it. It's the only thing that makes sense. Neighbors wouldn't think anything strange about seeing her out and about. It's weird that she would break into her friends' houses and handle their stuff, and then steal their stuff," I said.

"Hannah, it couldn't be Louise!" Mom said. I hadn't realized she was listening.

"But there's an obvious feng shui connection here," I said.

"Louise embraces many philosophies and beliefs, just like we all do. Just because she is studying feng shui doesn't mean she is presumptuous enough to feng shui someone's house without their knowledge. And I can't believe I'm using 'feng shui' as a verb," Mom said.

She might have said something after that, but I really couldn't hear her any longer. The sound inside the Convention Center was deafening. Hundreds of people talking all at once in a cavernous space that seemed to amplify sound. All four of the local TV stations had camera crews there ready to capture individuals' hopes and dreams for their items. I imagined that every station would start the story with images of the crowds and long lines, and then they'd talk about how many people were there and how long we waited in line. People watching at home would probably feel a little sorry for us because most of us would spend so much time only to find our items were worthless, at least in terms of monetary value.

Mom lifted her lamp-holding arm again, this time waving to her friend Mary Perez from KOMO TV. Mary waved back, imitating Mom's lamp-lifting gesture. I was definitely going to watch the news tonight. Mary is the kind of reporter who will find the most interesting story of the day. Two of her most interesting stories featured our first two big cases in Belltown and on Portage Bay. Yep. Mary always did the best stories.

Our instructions said to stay in line until the first-round appraisal crew came by to get some general information and take a quick photo. The first-round appraiser we got didn't seem to be enjoying his job very much.

"Name? Number? Object?" He wrote down just the basics and then took a picture with a digital camera.

"That's it? My future will be decided by that guy?" Lily whined.

I'd read up on how the show worked, so I wasn't as worried. "They're going to send the digital image to an appraiser who specializes in a particular area. If the item looks intriguing to that appraiser, our number will be posted on the big digital screen over there."

"But he just had me hold the brooch in my hand. He didn't get a picture of me," Lily whined. I knew she was kidding. She's a drama queen to be sure, but she's not conceited or unreasonable.

We found a place to sit down and eat our lunches. I looked around for Georgia and Louise, but I didn't see them. I certainly didn't see Georgia before I practically ran into her, head to head, on the way to the bathroom.

"Hi, Georgia," I said. "I don't know if you remember me. My name is Hannah. I live across the street from Louise," I said. Look at me! Friendly girl with grown-up manners!

"Oh, hey, I thought you looked familiar. Nice to see you again. My name's Georgia. Wait. You already knew that. My last name is Smith. Georgia Smith. Hey, would you be willing to watch my box while I go into the bathroom? I can't figure out any way to keep Louise's and my things safe and take care of business, if you know what I mean."

Georgia eased the box onto the floor. I said I was happy to keep an eye on things. I'd be even happier if I knew what kinds of "things" I was watching (but I

111

didn't actually say that part). I bent over to look inside, but all I could see was a bunch of bubble wrap and tissue paper. I poked around a bit, but everything was wrapped tight. I was tempted to try to unwrap the items a bit, but it was too risky.

"Thanks so much," Georgia said when she came back out.

"No problem," I said. "What did you bring here today?" I asked. I sounded exactly like Marcia Wellstone, host of *Antiques Caravan*.

"Me? Oh, just a . . . bowl. A salad bowl. My uncle found it at a Goodwill somewhere in Michigan," she said.

A bowl, eh?

"What kind of bowl? Ceramic? Glass?" I inquired. I was really thinking: a Chihuly bowl? But that was crazy. A blown-glass bowl by Dale Chihuly was certainly not an antique.

"Ceramic. What about you? Did you bring something? Or are you here with your parents?"

"I brought a Ming Dynasty brush pot my grandfather gave me," I said, realizing, of course, that it could be imitation. "My mom is here, too. She's hauling some old lamp around. She also brought a ton of food, so come find us if you want to eat."

"Right. I'll do that. Thanks again for keeping an eye on my . . . bowl," she said as she lifted the box and walked away.

"Good-bye," she called over her shoulder. I stood as if rooted to the carpet. I could wait a few seconds and head in the same direction, following her. I wanted to know what was in the box.

Unfortunately, I had something else I needed to take care of first. At that moment I needed to go to the bathroom.

## CHAPTER 21

"I TOLD YOU THOSE NUMBERS WERE LUCKY!" LILY SQUEALED AS THE digital board showed that numbers 433, 434, and 435 were to go on to the next stage.

The guy who had checked us in told us where to go if our numbers were posted.

"It looks like we need to go to three different areas," Mom said. "How do you girls want to do this?"

"I can go alone," I said. I held up my cell phone, in anticipation of Mom's question, which would most certainly be "Do you have your cell phone?," followed by "Is your cell phone fully charged?" Yes, and yes again.

"Okay, *call* me if it seems they're going to continue with your pot, and I'll run right over," Mom said.

I headed over to a section labeled "Asian Art."

"I'll need your release, signed by someone over eighteen, like a parent, and your registration form," a girl said at the entrance to the section. I handed her my paperwork, completed and signed by my mom, and she checked me off a list.

"Hello, what's your name?"

I was surprised to see that Marcia Wellstone, the main host of *Antiques Caravan*, was speaking to me. I remembered I'd seen her talking about Chinese art and artifacts on the show before. This must be her area of expertise, on top of being the main host. Suddenly everything lit up, and I knew the cameras were rolling. Man, once they start moving on this they really move fast. There wasn't any time to call Mom.

"I'm Hannah," I said.

"It's wonderful to meet you here in Seattle, Hannah," Marcia said. "What do you have here today?"

I held out my hands with the brush pot and brush rest.

"Let's put them on the table here. What can you tell me about these pieces?"

I wondered if I'd perhaps lost the ability to talk, now that there was a chance this might be on TV. Lily and I had been on a TV show called *Dockside Blues* last summer, but no matter how important Lily tries to make it sound, we were still just extras. I'd never actually had to talk.

"This is a porcelain Chinese brush pot that my grandfather gave me. It was designed to hold calligraphy brushes. And this coordinating piece is where one would rest his or her brush when taking a break." Whoa! Look at me! I rattled that off like some sort of expert. I felt as if I were outside my body watching as someone else took over.

"Both pieces are quite lovely, aren't they? And it seems that they were indeed intended as a set. Do you know anything about the age or the style?" Marcia asked.

Here I go again: "I think this style of pottery is from the Ming Dynasty, which would mean it was made somewhere between 1368 and 1643. I don't actually know if it's real. It could be an imitation of something from the Ming Dynasty."

"Your knowledge is quite impressive," Marcia said. She smiled. She seemed nice, and all of a sudden I felt completely relaxed. "Did your grandfather tell you all of this?"

"No, actually I went to the library and looked it up in *Kovels*'," I said.

"That would be *Kovels' Antiques and Collectibles*, an excellent resource," she said. I could tell she was clarifying my source in case we really ended up on

TV. The title of the book would probably appear on screen, too. "Hannah, your research at the library has certainly paid off. These pieces are, in fact, from the Ming Dynasty. The color at the top tells me that these were created in the later part of that dynasty, probably between 1612 and 1624."

I saw that my mom had come into our section. Maybe she had a hunch that the bright lights meant they'd chosen me.

"Is your grandfather of Chinese descent?" Marcia asked.

"No, he wasn't. He's my mom's dad," I said, pointing to Mom.

"Great! Let's get Hannah's mom in this story," Marcia said. They exchanged quick handshakes and introductions.

"So these items were a gift from your father?" Marcia prompted Mom.

"Yes. He bought them for Hannah before she was born. He died several months before I actually went to China to bring her home. But my dad knew she was coming, and he knew she would be a much-loved girl," Mom said. Uh-oh. She was choking up. This always happened when she talked about her dad and how he died before he met me.

"He left me a note that said he knew I'd find my way in the world artistically," I said, to divert some attention from Mom, in case she completely blubbered.

"That's a lovely story. Do you use these items?"

"I do use them. I'm an artist, just like my grandfather predicted," I said.

"Excellent. Well, Hannah and Maggie, these items are authentic, but they are not rare. The value for the brush pot is $545, and $230 for the brush rest. Are you going to hang on to them?" Marcia asked.

"Absolutely. I'm keeping these forever," I said.

"I'm sure you'll make good use of them and take good care of them. Thank you so much for sharing your story with *Antiques Caravan*."

The lights turned off. Instantly things felt dark and cold. I've been around TV cameras and lights enough to know that it always feels that way once the harsh, bright lights go away.

"That really was great. Thank you so much!" Marcia said. "I really enjoyed this segment. We'll let you know when it will air."

## CHAPTER 22

**"DID YOU HEAR THAT?" I ASKED MOM WHEN THE CREW HAD MOVED ON TO** someone else. "She didn't say *if* the segment airs, she said she'll let us know *when* it will air. As if it's a done thing!"

"You were great!" Lily rushed up to me.

"You saw it?" I asked.

"Yeah, we have some time to kill before they get to us," Lily said.

"How about you, Mom? What's up with the lamp?"

"Who cares? I'm just so thrilled about your fame," she said.

"Does that mean they weren't interested in the lamp?" I asked "You've been hauling it around for nothing?"

"I'll have you know that they were quite interested in the lamp. The first round estimate is that it's worth more than $4,000. But I don't have any emotional attachment to this lamp, and I have a bit of an attachment to you. I'm sure Happy and Frank don't mind. They probably know exactly how much the lamp is worth anyway," Mom said.

"Maybe that's exactly how much they paid for it," Lily said.

"Anyway, I'm glad I gave up my spot," Mom said. She gave me a big hug.

Her devotion to me also meant she'd be lugging that lamp around for the rest of the day.

The TV lights were back on in our section.

"Let's watch this next one," Mom whispered.

"It's Louise!" I hadn't realized she was in the same section I was. Marcia Wellstone had already gone through the introductions before we got close enough to clearly see and hear everything.

"I understand you're quite knowledgeable about feng shui, the Chinese practice of placement and arrangement of space, which is believed to achieve harmony with the environment," Marcia said.

"I'm studying feng shui, and I make it a part of my daily life in my work and living spaces. But I believe it will be a lifelong study. There is so much to learn," Louise said. "It is a discrete system involving a mix of geographical, philosophical, mathematical, aesthetic, and astrological ideas. Feng means 'wind,' and shui translates to 'water.'"

"Are there a few basics you could give us now?" Marcia prompted.

"It's quite complex, and Americans tend to make light of it. But in general, color dictates much of what happens in a room. Red is a creative, energetic color and is best used on a southern wall. If you have a creative job, you might consider a red southern wall in your work space. If you work at home, you should make sure the toilet lid stays closed, especially if it's in a straight line from an outside exit. Otherwise money that comes into your home might be flushed away."

Mom put her hand on my arm as if to keep me from jumping up and down while pointing and screaming "Ah-ha! *You* are the culprit!"—which is exactly what I wanted to do. I knew it all along, and I wanted to make that known, too. Well, almost all along. Now the two specific examples Louise gave were exactly what she had done to houses on Millionaire's Row. Okay. She hadn't exactly painted a wall red, but there were those paint chips taped up to a southern wall in one of those big brick houses. Closing the toilet lid in Jodi and Charlie's house had deprived their animals of an extra water source, but Louise thought it was important for them to have it closed.

"Anything that applies to *Antiques Caravan*?" Marcia asked Louise.

"Definitely. You should know the history of the objects in your home. If a piece of furniture or an artifact was stolen or was once owned by someone who went bankrupt or otherwise met bad fortune, you may want to reconsider having that item in your home," Louise said.

"Let's talk about the item you brought from your home," Marcia said. "What can you tell us?"

I hadn't paid much attention to the bowl that was on the table next to Louise. She picked it up and I still couldn't tell what was significant about it. It looked a little like a bowl I made for Mother's Day in fourth grade. It was unglazed terra cotta with a zigzag design painted or etched on the perimeter.

"From what I've been told, this is early Chinese painted pottery, possibly as old as 2000 B.C. It's hand modeled, and the walls appear to be built by cording. As you can see, it's only about six inches in diameter and so was probably used in the home for food or beverage," she explained.

"Looks like you can have my job," Marcia said with a laugh. "You're absolutely right. This is a Neolithic pottery bowl, Majiayao Yangshao Culture, from the Machang phase, which places it somewhere between 2000 and 2300 B.C., although I have a hunch it's closer to the 2000 B.C. mark, which, of course, is quite impressive. The condition is good. There are a few minor chips to the rim, but they're quite minor and don't detract from the significance of this rare piece. May I ask how you came to have this?"

I was grinding my teeth. She probably stole it from one of our neighbors.

"It was a gift from my ex-husband," Louise said. She seemed to catch something in Marcia's face. Louise laughed and quickly added, "My ex-husband and I remain dear friends, and I don't believe there's any negative energy associated with how this piece came into my possession."

A likely story, I thought.

"Any idea of the value?" Marcia asked. Louise shook her head no.

When Marcia gave the estimated value, there was a gasp from the crowd. It was definitely an amount worth gasping over. Staggering. I can't even repeat it because it blows my mind.

And to think Louise had probably stolen it from the rightful owners.

The TV lights turned off and several people rushed to speak with Louise and Marcia. Maybe she'd sell it before she left the building.

**CHAPTER 23**

MOM WAS KEEPING A TIGHT LEASH ON ME, SO TO SPEAK, TRYING TO KEEP me from getting involved in Louise's—or whoever it rightfully belonged to—bowl.

"Louise seems so happy right now. Maybe we can just leave her alone for a while," Mom said. "Besides, she said her former husband gave her the bowl. She obviously knows quite a bit about its history."

I wasn't convinced.

If I couldn't get to the truth today, I knew it would come out when *Antiques Caravan* aired. Or maybe this part wouldn't air. I'd read that the *Caravan* research team thoroughly researched each item before it was featured on the TV program. When the show first started years ago, they'd featured a painting that had been stolen from a private collector eighty years ago. The painting had fallen off the radar of those in the art-appraising world because the crime had happened so many years ago. But the much-loved painting was part of one family's history, and the great-grandniece of the owner recognized it on the air. Ever since, *Antiques Caravan* had scrupulously researched each item mentioned or even shown in passing.

That was all reassuring, but it sure would be a lot more fun if I exposed Louise and her crime today.

Still, I went along with Mom and hoped I'd convinced her that I was being mellow about all this. We wandered around for another ninety minutes, waiting for Lily's brooch to be appraised. We eavesdropped on other people's appraisals and even talked to people about their treasures.

"Let's look in here. I love Art Nouveau," Mom said.

Georgia was standing behind a table. There were two objects on the table. One was a red glass bowl. The other was a blue vase.

Libby's blue vase.


"That's . . . " I started to say to Mom, but a guy with a headset on called out, "Quiet on the set." The lights came up, focused on Georgia. "Five, four," the guy with the headset was counting down, "three, two, one . . . "

"You have two quite distinct items here, so I've

asked my colleague to join me," a man in a bow tie said. "Let's start with this vase. What can you tell us about this vase?"

"I don't actually know that much. My grandfather gave it to me. He died before I was born. He left it, along with a note, with my mother to give to me," she said. Hey, wait a minute! That's my story. Had she seen my segment and decided to use my story as her own? That would make sense, since she couldn't have her own story because the vase wasn't hers.

"You have no idea of the age or its origins?" bow-tie man asked.

"No . . . " she stammered. Origins? I'll tell you the origins! I scrawled a note to Mom: LIBBY'S VASE!!!!

Mom scrawled, "Sure?"

"Absolutely," I wrote, and underlined it three times.

Bow-tie man was talking about Art Nouveau something or other. Mom motioned that she was going to go make a phone call. I hoped she was calling the police.

"It's value is $3,200," bow-tie man finished. "But what we really want to talk with you about today is this magnificent iridescent piece of Louis Comfort Tiffany glass."

There was a gasp behind me. The camera guy and the sound woman glared at me. Hey, it wasn't me! I turned around to face Louise. Her eyes were huge, her eyebrows raised, and her hand clasped over her mouth as if to keep herself from screaming.

Ah-ha! *You* are the culprit! I wanted to say it out loud, but I knew I couldn't. I mean, I could say it out loud, but I didn't want to get in trouble with those TV folks. I just didn't have the guts to do it. If only Lily was here. She'd seize this opportunity to be on national television and catch a culprit.

Clearly, Louise and Georgia had been working together. Clearly, Louise had no idea that Georgia was going to come on *Antiques Caravan* with items the two had stolen in their feng shui scam. I wasn't sure who owned that Tiffany glass piece, but it was undoubtedly someone on Millionaire's Row.

"Tiffany? Really?" Georgia said.

"You seem surprised. What can you tell us about this bowl?"

"It's . . . it's also from my grandfather. It's quite old," Georgia said.

"I'd say this is from about 1910. Our culture today often hears about Tiffany glass lamps. Reproductions of the jewel-toned lamps are everywhere," the man said. "In fact, the reproductions can be rather inexpensive."

Georgia nodded.

"An authentic Tiffany lamp could be several thousand dollars," he said. "Excuse me, I meant to say a Louis Tiffany lamp could be worth several *hundred* thousand dollars. A Magnolia floor lamp has been valued at $1.5 million."

"Really?" Georgia stammered with excitement.

"Indeed." He held the bowl up to the light. "This is Favrile, a type of glass process patented by Tiffany in 1880. Different colors of glass are mixed together while hot. Vases and bowls may not be as valuable as the lamps . . . " the man paused.

"Really?" Georgia said again, the disappointment clear in her voice.

"A vase could range from $60,000 or more . . . " he began, but Georgia interrupted him.

"Really!"

"Yes, as I was saying, ranging from $60,000 to $80,000 on the high end, and a couple of thousand dollars on the low end."

I waited for Georgia to say "really" again. She said nothing. She looked like she was holding her breath, waiting for the verdict.

"Many of these pieces are unmarked. Tiffany pieces have been handed down in families, and people haven't even realized what they had. Did your family know?"

"We had no idea," Georgia said. "We always took special care of it, but that's just because it seemed fragile. And beautiful. It's obviously beautifully crafted."

"Indeed. Beautifully crafted. Many bowls like this were crafted around 1902, but few survived, possibly because people didn't realize they were Tiffany. I'd value this piece at $22,000 to $24,000."

"Oh, my!" Georgia said, her face flushing. "My grandmother, I mean grandfather, would be so excited!"

"So would my aunt," Louise practically hissed from behind us. "Although Aunt Betty always knew that bowl was Tiffany."

"You mean it's yours?" I asked incredulously.

Louise nodded. "Absolutely. That little thieving . . . thief!"

"But aren't . . . aren't you . . . ?" now I was the one faltering.

"The feng shui culprit? Yes. The thief? No."

And I believed her.

## CHAPTER 24

"WILL YOU ENTERTAIN OFFERS FOR THIS EXQUISITE TIFFANY STUDIOS bowl, or do you intend to keep it in the family?" the appraiser asked.

Georgia was beaming. "I'm definitely open to any offers."

I'll just bet she is.

"Quick! Your phone!" I said to Mom, holding out my hand. Only my mom wasn't back.

Louise handed me hers. Excellent. It was a camera phone. I maneuvered my way through the crowd so I could get photographs of Libby's vase and Louise's bowl. I was too far away to photograph it really well, but I gave it a shot anyway.

"Come on!" I motioned to Louise. She stood in the back of the crowd, frozen. As I turned back to Georgia, two security guards came and escorted her away. People in black polo shirts with the *Antiques*

*Caravan* logo whisked in to protect the fragile—and valuable—items.

"Louise, let's follow them," I urged her.

"I wonder if I should just let it go," she said softly. "It's all my fault after all."

"It's not your fault if she stole something from you. Did you see that blue vase she had? I'm sure that was Libby's vase. And I bet Mark and Tom's Chihuly bowl is in that box of hers somewhere, if not on her dining room table," I said. Louise looked years older and inches smaller to me. She looked sad to the core.

"Louise, I should apologize to you. I thought you were the feng shui thief. I was sure it was you breaking into houses and trying to make the energy flow better through feng shui," I said.

"I thought I was helping them," she said softly. "I had no idea people would see it as an intrusion. I thought they'd welcome the improvements in their living spaces and what that can bring to their lives. Georgia was studying with me. I thought she was helping me. But ... "

Mom came back just then.

"What did the police say?" I asked Mom. "Do we need to stall Georgia? Tail her?"

"I didn't call the police. I would have sounded like

a crackpot. I called Libby, hoping she would call the police with the case number. But I didn't reach her."

"Maybe we should bring Louise and go backstage to see if we can confront Georgia now," I said

"Louise? Is she still here?" Mom asked.

I looked around and realized that she wasn't.

She had probably taken off when she heard the word *police*.

MOM AND I LOOKED AROUND FOR LOUISE. WE DIDN'T SEE HER. GEORGIA and her entourage of *Antiques Caravan* staff people had disappeared, too. The security guards probably thought they were keeping the bowl safe from thieves. That was kind of a twisted joke.

"We made it on TV!" Lily squealed, coming up behind us. "I wish you could have seen it. We were magnificent."

"Lily, we don't have absolute confirmation that they're using us," her mom said. She was beaming, too. There was so much energy buzzing around this whole *Antiques Caravan* setup. It would be impossible not to get caught up in it. And who doesn't love the idea of being on television?

"Who are you looking for?" Lily asked. "Hoping for another shot of fame today?"

But I didn't have time to explain. "Excuse me," I

said to an official-looking person with a clipboard and the standard black *Antiques Caravan* T-shirt. "Do you know where we could find Ms. Smith? She was the one who was just here with that glass bowl," I asked the member of the crew.

"I believe she went back to our office area to entertain offers on her Tiffany piece, or, as you say, that glass bowl," he replied.

"We'd like to make an offer," my mom said. Yay, Mom! The man looked her up and down, as if deciding she had expensive enough shoes to be able to make an offer to Ms. Smith. Mom purposefully moved the lamp to a different position. She'd been lugging that thing around all day and now it was finally paying off. She held it confidently, as if she'd just purchased it from someone. If you can buy a $4,000 lamp—an ugly $4,000 lamp—on the spur of the moment, maybe you can buy something ten times that much, too.

"Yes, then, come with me." We all started following him. He stopped abruptly and turned. "Just two of you, please."

Obviously that would be Mom and me. Lily stepped forward, but I elbowed her back. "I'll go, Mom. I'll help carry my new bedside lamp," I said, trying to sound like a sweet but spoiled rich kid.

The office area was nothing fancy. Not at all. There were card tables and stacks of paper, boxes of files, computers with a zillion wires tangled together.

"Please write your offer on this form," the man said. "Ms. Smith will evaluate all offers in a few minutes. We'll be taping her again as she looks at the offers. It's a new segment for the show."

I grabbed the form from Mom.

"Manners, Hannah!" she scolded.

"My apologies. I assure you I can take care of this for you, Ms. West," I said formally.

Instead of writing a dollar amount, I wrote, "Hi, Georgia! Did you know my neighbor Libby has a vase exactly like that blue one? Only thing is, hers was stolen. So was Louise's red Tiffany bowl." I signed it, "Love, Hannah," which I thought was a nice friendly touch.

The camera crew came in. A makeup person powdered Georgia's nose and put a microphone on the collar of her shirt. Georgia smoothed her hair and quickly put on lipstick. They positioned both the vase and the bowl next to her.

"Now, as you examine the offers, please feel free to tell us as much or as little as you'd like," Marcia Wellstone coached Georgia.

Georgia began opening envelopes and pulling out each form. She looked extremely serious as she read the first one, then smiled and said, "This is a *very* good offer." She smoothed the form and put it to her right. She opened the second one and, again, looked at it intently. "A good offer, but a bit lower." She put it to the left. Envelope three brought "Another *very* good offer" and earned a place in the pile on the right. Envelope four went to the left; envelope five to the right. She spent more time on the form in envelope six. No smiles this time. She looked around anxiously until she spotted me. I waved. It was a friendly wave. After all, I'd signed the note "Love, Hannah."

Our envelope didn't make it into either pile. Georgia tossed it aside and in one swift move she scooped up Libby's blue vase and Louise's Tiffany bowl. No time for bubble wrap to protect the items. No time to comment on the contents of our note. Georgia bolted out of the makeshift office and into the halls of the Convention Center.

Mom and I followed her out, winding our way through a maze of office chairs and boxes.

"There!" I said, pointing to Georgia once we were out on the Convention Center floor.

"Watch it! Please!" a man snapped at us. Just in

time, too. I'd almost plowed into the carved wood bench he and another man were carrying.

"Sorry!" I said, dodging to the right to keep moving.

"Slow down!" a woman said. She pushed a cart with a wingback chair.

This time I dodged to the left.

"This way!" Lily said. "She came cruising right by us. Let's go!"

We didn't find her.

Libby's vase was gone. Louise's bowl was gone.

Worse, now Louise and Georgia were gone, too.

## CHAPTER 26

IT WAS PRETTY ANTICLIMACTIC TO COME HOME AFTER THAT CRAZY DAY. No TV cameras in the kitchen waiting to interview us. No thieves in the hallways for us to track. Mom had called and left messages for Libby and for Louise. She refused to let me call the police directly until we had talked with our neighbors.

Libby didn't have a chance to call us back until late afternoon. We told her everything and then brought our photos over to her house. She was looking for the case number to reference for when she called the police again.

"I don't know how seriously they'll take me," she said. "There must be all kinds of people who claim that something they saw on *Antiques Caravan* is really theirs and was stolen."

But this was different. Libby had reported it stolen *before* it appeared on *Antiques Caravan*.

"You really should call the police right away," Calvin said. As if on cue, Rachel brought the phone to her mom.

Turns out the police saw it my way this time. Sort of. They agreed that because the vase had been reported stolen *before* I saw it at the TV taping, it was worth looking into. Two things I hadn't expected: They didn't exactly trust my claim that it was absolutely the same vase (even when I told them I had photographic evidence) and, worst of all, they wondered why a kid like me had such interest in a stolen vase in the first place.

"You seem to have quite a bit of interest in this vessel," an officer said to me. Mom and I stayed at Libby's house until the police came. Lily and her mom had gone home, but with a sincere offer to vouch for my astute eye for details.

"I know. It's weird, isn't it?" I said, hoping that agreeing with police officers made me seem like a cooperative witness, rather than a possible culprit. "I sketched it a couple of times when I was babysitting Rachel. That's why I know it so well."

I offered my sketchbook to the closest officer.

As she looked at it, Rachel brought me a crayon drawing she'd done of the blue vase, too.

"This is excellent," I said, giving her a hug.

"I also have photos of the same vase at the *Antiques Caravan*," I said. "Oh, wait. I don't." I forgot that I borrowed Louise's camera phone to snap a couple images of Georgia with the vase and the bowl.

"Photos of the little glass doodad you mentioned would be helpful," one of the officers said.

"Actually, it's a bit more than a glass doodad. It's a 1910 Louis Tiffany glass bowl," I said.

"Once again, you seem to know quite a lot about these valuable items."

"Yes," I answered. What else could I say? Maybe this officer thought I was suspicious, but at least I'm always honest.

"Excuse me, I just heard a knock at our front door," Libby said. A few seconds later she was back.

"Officers, this is our neighbor Louise Zirkowski, the owner of the missing red bowl," Libby said as Louise came into the room.

"Are you ready to report this item as stolen?" one officer asked. She nodded. They handed her forms. She, in turn, handed them a file folder with several pieces of paper in it.

"I've photocopied my family's bill of sale for the

bowl. It's dated 1903. There are also photographs of the piece as well as a description from when we had it insured," she said. "I also want to give you this." She handed them one more piece of paper. "This is the information on Georgia Smith. She was an apprentice with me, studying feng shui. We believe she has the items."

I smiled at Louise to show my support. I was also trying to be supportive so she'd tell a little more.

"And . . . " I prompted. Still nothing. "And wasn't there something more about feng shui you said you were going to tell us all?"

"Yes, I suppose there is. Thank you, Hannah, for keeping me on the right track. Officers, you may have information on another case from Fourteenth Avenue East. Some of my neighbors reported someone coming into—breaking into—their homes and . . . rearranging things. In some cases, things were tidied up. In other cases, items were left, such as a bowl of satsumas." Louise looked pointedly at the bowl of satsumas on Libby's dining room table.

The officers didn't look too interested in this discussion. It was pretty clear that the neighbors at the Block Watch meeting had been right. The police had never taken the complaints that seriously to begin with.

"The thing is . . . I'm the culprit in that one," Louise said.

I couldn't believe she said "culprit"! All those times I'd looked at her and thought: Ah-ha! You are the culprit!

"You're the one who broke into homes?" one officer said. She looked skeptical. Perhaps she thought Louise was covering for someone else.

"Oh, no! I didn't break anything, or break *into* anything," Louise said. "I have keys to most of the houses on the street. I often water plants and feed cats when people are away. We're a friendly neighborhood."

"Did the neighbors know you were going to use the key at times they hadn't specified? I assume you have keys to check on plants while they're on vacation, take in the mail, that sort of thing. That's quite different from entering in the middle of the day and messing up someone's belongings."

"Messing up? I wasn't messing anything up. I was just instilling some feng shui principles into their living spaces," Louise said. She sounded humble, and even a little bit ashamed.

"I believe that still constitutes breaking and entering," one officer said. He looked at the other, as if waiting for her agreement. She nodded. "We'll get back to you on that. I'm not sure what charges we'll press. In the meantime, it looks like we need to track down one Georgia Smith."

"You might be able to catch her at the Yogini Center. She told me earlier she was planning on going to the four o'clock vinyasa class," Louise said.

The officers looked at her and shook their heads before leaving the house.

"Louise, I don't understand how you think that you were doing people a favor," Libby said gently.

"I don't think that anymore," she said. Then she let out a deep sigh. "I thought people would know right away that it was me. I've been talking nonstop about feng shui, and I left those calming stones as gifts, and as a sort of calling card. But Hannah here made me realize that what I'd done was a bit . . . creepy, to say the least." She smiled at me. I, of course, had to smile back. Because once again a twelve-year-old had set a clueless adult straight.

The phone rang, and Calvin raced Rachel to answer it. They came back into the dining room, with Rachel riding on her dad's shoulders.

"All taken care of," Rachel said. "The police say a-okay."

We looked at Calvin for an interpretation. "That was the police. They picked up Georgia. They met her as she was coming out of her yoga class. She was carrying a yoga mat, and a box with a vase and one glass bowl. Another glass bowl—a more modern blown-glass one—was found in the backseat of her car. Sounds like it's Mark and Tom's missing Chihuly bowl."

## CHAPTER 27

You're invited to a special screening of
*Antiques Caravan*
Starring Hannah West and Lily Shannon
Friday at seven o'clock in the evening
at Libby and Calvin Greenfield's house
Showtime begins promptly at eight p.m.
BYOD (Bring Your Own Dog)

**YOU CAN'T SAY THE WORD *PARTY* AROUND A FOUR-YEAR-OLD UNLESS YOU**
fully intend to follow through. When Libby and Calvin
mentioned they wanted to have a party the night that
*Antiques Caravan* aired, Rachel immediately started
talking party plans.

Libby insisted that Mom and I invite whoever we
wanted. Mom had agreed, but only on the condition
that Libby let her help out with the hostessing duties.
Once that was agreed to, Mom and I realized that it

would be a nice way to bring together the people whom we had met during our different house-sitting gigs.

As we went over the guest list with Libby, Rachel had begged for stories about each person. She especially wanted stories about their dogs. She particularly liked the story about Ruff, the cairn terrier who had played a part in my first case.

"I want to meet Ruff," Rachel announced. "Can we invite Ruff?" she asked her parents.

Calvin hesitated, but Libby rushed in with a yes.

"We don't have to invite Ruff," I said gently to Rachel. "We have all the dog we need right here with Izzie."

"Izzie wants to invite Ruff! Izzie wants all the dogs to come!" Rachel said. "Can they, Mommy? Can the dogs come?"

This time Libby hesitated. "I guess so," she said.

"Yippee!" Rachel said.

Calvin gave Libby one of those "What have you got us into?" looks. Mom often sent that same kind of look my way.

"Is Louise coming?" Libby asked Mom on the night of the party. They were in the kitchen slicing tomatoes and chopping basil.

"She said she'd rather not," Mom said. "Something about how she's taking a break from using electronic devices."

"Maybe the whole ordeal is still painful for her," Libby said.

"Maybe she didn't think she should come without a dog of her own," Lily said.

The doorbell rang, and things got a little crazy as the party guests and their dogs arrived. Dorothy Powers and her cairn terrier, Ruff, were the first to arrive. Mom and I met Dorothy when we were house-sitting in the Belltown Towers.

Mango, a labradoodle we'd taken care of on a houseboat last summer, arrived with his owner, Jake Heard, and his neighbor, Alice Campbell. Elvis, a basset hound, made his entrance, dragging his owner, Piper Christensen, behind him. We'd taken care of Elvis in Fremont. Not far behind Elvis was Scooter, a big shaggy dog from Fremont, with his owner, Benito.

"Dad couldn't come," Benito said. "He's on a case. By the way, he said to tell you congrats on your big case." Ben's dad is a private detective. I felt proud that someone like Tom Campo recognized my sleuthing skills.

"Maybe Hannah can give your dad some tips," Lily offered.

"Hannah, so nice to see you!" Ben's grandfather, Mack Pappas, shook my hand. He took off the old-fashioned hat he almost always wore and placed it on the table in the entryway.

Mom's friend Nina came with another artist, James, and their friend Polly Summers. The last guest to arrive was Jordan Walsh. I had gotten to know Jordan during our first case. I hadn't expected that we'd end up as friends, but it just worked out that way. Now we have Japanese and art together, and we're partners on a project on artists for our U.S. history class. Jordan, Lily, and I even eat lunch together every day at school.

Mom was in her waitress mode, making sure everyone had snacks and drinks. Calvin made sure everyone had a comfortable place to sit where they could see the TV. That second part wasn't really a problem, since the TV was so huge.

"It's going to start! It's going to start! Wee-wooh, wee-wooh!" Rachel was wearing her fire chief outfit again. Her fire-engine imitation made everyone laugh, but they quieted down as the theme music for *Antiques Caravan* started. The camera scanned the Seattle skyline as the music faded.

"There I am!" Rachel squealed. She somehow picked her tiny little red fire chief hat out of the throng of people along the sidewalk as the lead *Antiques Caravan* truck came down Fourteenth Avenue.

"There I am again!" Rachel squealed. "Look at me! I'm here, and I'm there!" She stood next to the TV, pointing to herself in her fire chief outfit, and then pointing to herself onscreen in her fire chief outfit. "I'm double! I'm twins!"

"We'd love to have two of you," her dad said.

The next close-up was of Lily in her circa 1906 outfit. I was right next to her, proudly wearing my cougar sweatshirt. "Grr!" Rachel said, giggling and pointing at me.

The TV showed the houses along Millionaire's Row, each one looking more stunning than the last, and then showed some highlights from Volunteer Park and the Seattle skyline at sunset.

I was the second person featured on the show. And let me tell you, it's really awful to watch yourself on TV. I don't sound the way I think I sound in real life.

"This is a porcelain Chinese brush pot that my grandfather gave me. It was designed to hold callig- raphy brushes. And this coordinating piece is where one would rest his or her brush when taking a break," I said to Marcia Wellstone. I glanced over at Mom. She was beaming with pride. I looked back at the TV. I guess

I looked okay. The red streaks in my hair looked good on air. And I was wearing my beloved long-sleeved yin-yang shirt, a step up from an ordinary T-shirt or my cougar sweatshirt.

"I hope I'm not too late for the party," Mary Perez, Mom's friend, entered the family room.

"You missed seeing the incredibly interesting me," I said. "Your loss."

"Believe me, Hannah, I saw you many times. I have this show practically memorized. You were all spectacular," she said. Mary did a big story for KOMO TV on the stolen items that showed up at the Antiques Caravan taping. The story was so juicy it had been picked up by the network and aired on national news. A part of the story would be part of tonight's show, too.

"And now, ladies and gentlemen . . . " Lily said, as the show moved to the jewelry segment.

"It's you!" Lily's brother, Zach, exclaimed. "You're dressed funny."

Lily shushed him. They weren't on long, but I have to admit that Lily was pretty relaxed and good on camera. She might be right about this acting thing.

Marcia Wellstone and Bradford Hines were in an elegant wood-panel office for the next segment.

"Something highly unusual happened when we were in Seattle," Marcia began.

"Yes, indeed, Marcia," Bradford Hines agreed. "As our viewers know, we thoroughly research each item that makes the final cut to be featured on our show. We don't want there to be any errors, nor should a piece be featured that has a questionable history."

The camera showed a close-up of Louise's bowl as Bradford Hines described the significance of Tiffany glass. The host also described Libby's blue vase, and showed it from several angles. Libby looked over at the vase on the table, as if to make sure it was right where it belonged.

"In an odd turn of events, it appears that both of these items were stolen from homes on Seattle's Millionaire's Row, the same street you saw at the beginning of tonight's program. Thanks to the work of Hannah West, the young woman we featured earlier with the Ming Dynasty brush pot, who also happens to live on Millionaire's Row, we were able to put all the pieces together. We asked reporter Mary Perez of Seattle to bring you the full details of the story."

We all watched as Mary went over the facts of the story. She interviewed Mom and me on camera about our involvement. Mom explained how we were professional house-sitters and so it's part of our job to look after our clients' belongings. Mom added that it often extended to looking after the neighbors' homes and well-being, too.

"Hannah's photography and sketching skills have figured into a few other incidents here in Seattle in the past year. Perhaps the police department should hire this seventh-grade artist permanently. From Seattle, this is Mary Perez."

"*You* are all over TV!" Lily said. She didn't sound jealous at all, and I knew she wasn't.

"I guess this is my fifteen minutes of fame?" I asked. No one answered. Everyone was talking at once.

Rachel handed me a new drawing.

"It's you and your mom and Vincent and Pollock," she said. "It's your family."

"I love it!" I said. And I meant it. In the drawing, my two goldfish were the same size as Mom's and my heads. Somehow, that seemed just perfect.

"I really like it here, but I hope people don't end up thinking that we actually live on Millionaire's Row," I whispered to Mom. "It totally blows my image as a struggling artist."

"Well, no matter what people think, I'll always be proud of you," Mom said, embracing me.

"Thanks," I said, hugging her back.

I looked around the room and was amazed to see so many people I knew in one place. I tried to stop all the corny thoughts percolating in my head. But these weren't just thoughts. They were feelings. And they were coming from my heart.

Suddenly, it didn't seem to matter at all that we didn't have a permanent address. Being surrounded by family and friends felt good. It felt like home.